Raven, Stay By Me

Raven,
Stay By Me

a novel by
L.W. van Keuren

JESPERSON PUBLISHING

Library and Archives Canada Cataloguing in Publication

Van Keuren, L. W., 1945 -
    Raven, stay by me / L. W. van Keuren.
ISBN 978-1-894377-30-0
1. Inuit – Juvenile fiction. 2. Ravens – Juvenile fiction. I. Title.
PZ7.V3263 Ra 2009   j813'.6   C2009-900836-X

We acknowledge the support of the Canada Council for the Arts which last year invested $20.1 million in writing and publishing throughout Canada. We acknowledge the financial support of the Government of Canada through the Book Publishing Industry Development Program for our publishing activities. We acknowledge the financial support of the Government of Newfoundland and Labrador through the department of Tourism, Culture and Recreation for our publishing activities.

Printed in Canada

Canada Council for the Arts   Conseil des Arts du Canada   Canada   Newfoundland Labrador

JESPERSON PUBLISHING
AN IMPRINT OF BREAKWATER BOOKS LTD.

P.O. Box 2188, 100 Water Street, St. John's, NL, A1C 6E6
www.breakwaterbooks.com

The artefacts included in this story
are real and are preserved in
historical collections, reminders of the Norse
explorations of the New World —
with the exception of one carved
figurine yet to be found.

Contents

PART 1   9

The Cloak Pin   10

Ship Fittings   25

The Birch Basket   36

PART 2   45

A Spindle Whorl   46

The Wooden Man   52

PART 3   71

The Stone Lamp   72

The Silver Penny   85

The Bone Needle   98

The Whetstone   115

PART 4   135

A Carved Figurine   136

During this winter there was much said in
Brattahlid about making plans to go to Vinland,
and it was declared that they would find good lands there.
This talk led to Karlsefni and Snorri preparing
their ship to seek Vinland during the summer.

Eirik the Red's Saga

Part 1

Kostbera's Dream:

A bear I saw enter,   *the roofbeams he broke,*
and he wielded his claws   *so that trembling we were;*
with his jaws seized he many,   *and fled was our might,*
so loud was the uproar   *not little to hear.*

Hogni interprets his wife's dream:

Now a storm is brewing   *and mad it blows swiftly.*
This dream of a snow bear   *means a gale from the east.*

The Greenland Ballad of Atli
(Atlamol En Groenlenzku)

Chapter One

The Cloak Pin

Early in the eleventh century, the coast of Newfoundland

Before she opened her eyes, Inga heard the sea. She felt rough, damp sand against her cheek. Behind her closed eyes, a memory flickered of her home in Greenland. There, every morning before she got up, she would hear the sea lulling her back to sleep and listen for the footsteps that told her Grandmother had left the cooking fire in the centre of the room to wake her.

Now Inga opened her eyes. She saw the sea before her: quiet, glimmering with morning sun. But her throat was sore. Her body ached. Yes, she remembered now. She was not at the farm in Greenland. There was no fragrance of a fire, no sound of beloved, familiar footsteps. She lay not on a warm fur spread on a sleeping bench, but on the cold pebbles of a beach. The great storm was over.

Beside her, a patch of shore grass shivered in the breeze. Around her lay a strange, frightening land.

Inga lay utterly still for several moments. She heard nothing. No voices, no skittering in the brush. She lifted her head. This land was unlike the first place, with its enormous dark stones, that they had seen from the ship. Those of her fellow passengers who had seen the lands to the west before said the first place was not Vinland, so they had sailed on farther south. Nor was Vinland the second place to come in sight, a land they called Markland – flat and forested with wide sand beaches. By then angry clouds prowled the horizon. There would be no going ashore in one of the small boats at Markland.

The Norse navigators chose to do what they always did. They knew their ships to be exceptionally swift, parting the waves with finely crafted prows. Leaving Markland behind, they tried to outrun the storm. They tried desperately.

Now, the world around Inga resembled neither the first place of the massive dark rocks nor the second, a forested land edged by wide-flung sandy beaches. This site was almost a flat plain, bumpy and green with grass and mosses. Stunted bushes and trees dotted the land, and a brook tumbled to the shore. She spotted heather and berry bushes, and these, at least, added cheer to the emptiness. Beyond the meadow lay low stony ridges and, farther on, dark, stunted trees. Forests crouched there, like wild things waiting to pounce.

"The boat," Inga whispered. She sat up. Where was the small boat she and Grandmother had used to flee the ship? Although her exhausted body longed to rest, Inga struggled to her knees. She felt the bruises on her legs, and her tunic was torn, her cloak sodden. Seaweed wound around her braids. A tender scrape reddened her arm.

This must be the morning *after* the storm, Inga told herself. Surely she and Grandmother could not have drifted longer than one night? That night had seemed so long while the pair of them clung to the little boat in the darkness, hearing the cold, foamy ocean sizzling around them and the rage of the storm. The small boat had rocked over the waves and the swell. Soon they no longer heard the heart-wrenching creak of the big ship's timbers or the hoarse cries of their companions. Only the roar of the wind. Only the roar of the sea.

But now this morning was dazzling with sun. At a distance from shore, white ripples of foam broke over a shoal. Down the coast, long fingers of land reached out into the sea. Nearly the entire inlet was shallow. Could she have crawled from the small boat when it went aground? Had she been tossed into the waves and swum here with the incoming tide? In her mind, that terrible night was a jumbled nightmare. She remembered nothing of their landing, and not even one plank of the boat lay on the sand to prove how she and Grandmother had come ashore.

Oh, she remembered well Grandmother seizing her hand and leaping from the ship into the little boat, one of those brought along for going ashore when the ship anchored. She and Grandmother had fallen hand-in-hand into the little boat, tumbling over the stern. They called to their friends to take the other boats and join them. But the waves pushed them farther and farther away from the ship. Then night fell. Inga remembered the awful darkness as they lay in the boat, gripping its ribs, horrified, numb, the sting of hail on their faces. That seemingly endless night had come to an end, after all. Here she was, safely on land, and she and Grandmother were safe.

Inga was hungry. Birds swirled above the ridges. Surely they were nesting there: and that meant eggs. Grandmother must have gone to collect some, she thought. Inga knew she must not roam far before Grandmother returned. Her body shook, not from cold but from fear. It was terrible to be alone — *all alone* — in this strange land, even for a few minutes.

With Grandmother near, she reminded herself, there was nothing to be afraid of. At home, people said that trolls ran when they heard Grandmother coming. Inga closed her eyes and tried to push the fear out of her body. After a while, she stopped shaking.

Her legs were stiff as she stumbled down to the sea. She cupped the cold, comforting salt water over her scrapes and scratches. Every few minutes, she glanced up to scan the shore. In what direction might the survivors be found? Together they might repair the ship, or, if not, build a house to keep them through the winter, if necessary, until friends from Greenland came to find them here in this new world. First, she and Grandmother must find the others.

"*Mormor!*" Inga called. "Grandmother!" The breeze blew her voice across the vacant land, like the voice of a faraway bird. "Grandmother!"

She heard nothing. Nothing but the sea.

Inga examined the shore in each direction. This time she noticed that the only footprints anywhere in the mud or the sand were her own. Grandmother must have been hunting food for some time. The tide had washed Grandmother's footprints away, so now Inga could not tell which way she had gone.

"*Mormor!* Grandmother!" she called again. "Grandmother!"

Nothing but the sea.

Inga searched for berries and hungrily stuffed those she found in her mouth. There were blueberries, few of them ripe yet, and crowberries and mountain cranberries, just like at home. Some berries she did not know, some with prickly briars, some in clusters of clear red fruit, sour but juicy. She hoped as the summer passed there would be berries the colour of glowing sunsets, whose broad white flowers had earlier covered the slopes. These were among the last to bear fruit, she knew, although she had never tasted them. Grandmother painted these on bowls and benches. They were cloudberries and grew in Norway where Grandmother had been born. She wondered if Grandmother had already found some growing here.

But the day wore on. Grandmother did not return. Inga sat on a rock, watching the shoreline. She had found a bit of vine and, pushing her braids aside, tried to mend her tunic. Then she sat for a time and did nothing. Suddenly her tears refused to stay where she wanted them to stay, so she let them trickle down her cheeks, warm and smarting. Her tears reminded her how scared she was, how terrifying the storm had been, how young a girl she was – eleven years old – in a vast, unfamiliar world. Then, at last, the tears stopped. They seemed to know that whether she was scared or not, she had things to do.

The sun arched westward. Grandmother still had not come. Inga thought about what she could try to do. At last, she placed several rocks one atop another, the largest she could carry at the bottom and the smallest on top. This was the way her people marked a spot on a long walk. On points of land, they often built piles of stones so tall that voyagers could see them as their ships passed. Any of the survivors walking by or traveling by boat would see her stones and know from this sign that one of their own was near. Then she set out to find Grandmother.

As she rounded each rocky point or climbed up a boulder, she could see a long distance down the shore, but she saw no one there. Sometimes fresh water lay cupped in a rock's surface. This water she ladled to her thirsty mouth. The land was uneven, the grass bristly, the red or golden moss sodden. Walking was not easy. She discovered mussels clinging to the sides of a tide pool. With a small pointed stone, she pried the shells open and hungrily ate the soft, salty flesh. She tried to notice exactly where she found mussels so she and Grandmother could look for more.

"*Mormor!* Grandmother!" she shouted, her hands arched around her mouth. "Grandmother!"

A frightening thought came to her. Suppose Grandmother lay hurt somewhere and had dragged herself into the brush to hide from bears and wolves. "Grandmother!" Inga called. She heard only birds on the ridges, wailing in the wind.

Inga walked on. From habit, she noticed patches of rushes and reeds and young, pliant saplings. From such things she knew how to weave baskets, fences and mats. As a tiny child she had first stood beside Grandmother who worked at her loom. As soon as Inga had been able to reach the threads, Grandmother had taught her to weave. Grandmother said her granddaughter had weaver's hands.

On and on, Inga searched. A gull screeched, darting up from behind a rock and veering away, so close she felt the rush of air from its wings. Then a thought came to her that made her angry at herself for her own foolishness. If Grandmother had been hurt and had crawled away from the tide, she would not have gone far. Instantly, Inga knew she must hurry back to where she had awakened on the sand. From there she must search in every direction, under each bush and gnarled tree, behind every rugged boulder.

She hurried as fast as her bruised body could take her. As she hastened, her thoughts were crowded with the faces of those she loved. She and Grandmother had come to this strange land to be near family. When Inga's father, Sigurd, had been lost at sea, her mother had gone to Iceland, hoping to convince her sister Kitta and her husband to come back to Greenland and join them at the farm. Inga's mother had left her with *Mormor*, her own mother. After three years, Inga found it hard to remember exactly what her mother's face looked like.

One day, at the farm in Greenland, Inga had stood by her grandmother as they emptied a snare of birds. Quietly, Grandmother had shared her secret thoughts with Inga. She feared Inga's Aunt Kitta and her husband would not come. She worried that Inga's mother might want to stay on with her sister in Iceland. Grandmother, like Inga, loved the farm in the fjords of Greenland. She loved to watch the goats playing in the pasture. She loved the crooked streams rollicking down to the shore. Like Inga, she loved to walk beside the sea through the summer slopes, sweet with berries.

Grandmother also had one son, Inga's Uncle Knut. He had been away in Vinland for two years by the time Grandmother had shared her secret thoughts with Inga. Uncle Knut and his friends had gone to cut trees for lumber they needed for building. His ship had not yet come back.

The spring had been cold and late, and the Greenlanders knew the Vinland voyagers would wait well into summer when the seas were safe again. Enormous icebergs and treacherous pack ice from the bays might yet be breaking loose. The more time passed, the more

Grandmother worried. Neither of her children — Inga's mother nor Uncle Knut — had come back, and Grandmother said that she herself was an old woman. One of her children must come home to take care of Inga. When she looked at her granddaughter, her eyes crinkled up with worry and care.

Then one of the leading men of the settlement, Arne Stefansson, announced a trip to Vinland to trade with the *skraelings*, the wild people who lived there. Grandmother hatched her plan. They must go on the voyage, find Uncle Knut and bring him back to the farm.

Arne Stefansson had been reluctant. He'd said to Grandmother, "Elina Eiriksdottir, this is a risky undertaking. Who knows what dangers we may encounter? This year the game may be scarce, the fishing poor, and the ice early. We may not be able to return right away. Winter will be long in that lonely place." Her head high, Grandmother said nothing. Arne Stefansson hesitated and went on gently, "True, we need women to manage the camp…but you are not the youngest of women." Grandmother lifted her chin higher. Inga knew what she would mutter, if she had not cared about spoiling their chances.

"Young twit," she would have scoffed. Instead she nodded, as if he were perfectly right. "I will take Ingibjorg," she replied. "She is a good cook and a hard worker. She has all the spirit of the young."

It was Arne Stefansson's turn to smile. "Ingibjorg Sigurdsdottir! She is a mere child!" That was too much. Grandmother did not let him have another word. She used them all herself.

"Inga sews well," she reminded at the last. "She mends a tear so that no thread seems to have been broken. She will keep your clothing mended. We will bring cloth and skins and make you new garments and boots during the winter. From me, you will have medicines when you are ill and the wisdom of...of maturity. And from Inga, freshness and energy that will make the winter short."

They had sailed as soon as the summer weather turned warm.

Yet Arne Stefansson had been right about many things. Out on the sea, sailing along alien, forbidding coasts, there were dangers. There was the danger of drift ice, scattered on the sea despite the summer mildness. Moreover, there were the dangers that live in people's minds.

Some of the voyagers scanned the dark, ominous swells for the terrible sea trolls *hafstrambar* and *margygyar*. When clouds gathered on the horizon, people whispered among themselves, lips trembling, about the trolls called *hafgerdingar*, the fierce beings that held storms and mountainous waves tightly in their grip until, in their awful wickedness, they let the storms go to crush the ships that dared to sail the seas those trolls claimed for themselves.

"Ignorant babble!" Arne Stefansson scoffed. "Old-fashioned nonsense."

Some voyagers replied that the *skraelings*, the wild people of Vinland, were real at least. "They are savage trolls," a grey-haired man told Grandmother. "I have seen them. Scarcely more than beasts, and with evil eyes! They have stone and ivory knives, devilish bows and arrows, and fiendish curses and spells. Only the foolish do not fear them!"

Arne Stefansson grinned. "Let's hope they bring fat bundles of fur with them to trade!" He turned his gaze to the waves and the wind, watching the direction the seabirds sped above the mast. Grandmother said Arne Stefansson was the most skilled of navigators, the best of captains.

A few days later the skies had turned grey. It looked as though Arne Stefansson's skills would be put to the test. The wind grew fitful. The first new land they met did not quiet the unrest. Stony mountains rose from the barren ground; massive rocks sloped to the shore. Glaciers jammed the crevices between mountains. Land like this they could find in Greenland, some complained. "Helluland," Arne Stefansson called this place: the land of the stone slabs.

The wind grew brisk, the air heavy. Some wanted to turn back, but the next day brightened a little and the wind was not so sharp. Inga breathed more calmly. Grandmother had spoken wisely of Arne Stefansson's prowess. Markland, the land of forests and sandy shores, waited not far ahead, their leader announced. "Ahh," some voices murmured when this new land came into view. These thick forests brought the promise of valuable timber. The wide smooth sands of the shore beckoned. Immediately some on board wanted to anchor there, take lumber from the woods and go no farther to find Vinland.

But they did not harvest the forests of Markland. At that very moment the storm struck. Furious, billowing clouds brought hail and lashing wind. Lightning crackling overhead, they sailed as fast as the swiftest seabird, trying to stay ahead of the storm. They headed south to whatever new lands lay beyond that place. A new terror filled the hearts of many. Would they flee too far and sail over the edge of the world into *ginnungagap*, the great abyss? A few shouted that they must find a sheltering bay or point.

"Madness!" Arne Stefansson bellowed into the wind. "We'd run aground and drown!" The more seasoned sailors among them agreed. Deep water was their friend. They must head for open sea and fly before the storm. They tried. Boldly they tried.

All that now seemed so long ago. After hours spent circling the spot where she had awakened that morning, Inga gave up searching for Grandmother. It did not appear that Grandmother lay injured anywhere nearby, as Inga had feared. She tried to be grateful for this, yet there had been no sign to encourage her: no footprint, no pile of stones, no broken twigs, no wisp of wool snagged on a briar.

Only for an instant did Inga dare think that the *skraelings* might have captured Grandmother. If so, then Grandmother was already in the land of ghosts, for the *skraelings* were not merciful people.

In the east the star of the evening glimmered with a pure and comforting light. Inga was so exhausted that her head wobbled with faintness, her feet stumbled. She could go no farther.

Inga slept deeply and awakened the next morning beside her stack of stones.

Yesterday, as she had trudged the shore, the breeze had dried her clothing. This morning her clothes were again damp, this time with dew. The sun rose on a sulky sky with little promise of warmth. Today she must find Grandmother. Grandmother would know what to do. For hours she searched in the opposite direction from her previous expedition, among the scraggly brush, the boulders and boggy patches. Surely Grandmother must have kept to the shore, hoping to meet others who had survived the storm. Inga even hoped she might see the prow of the ship, moored beyond the next point.

The sun mocked her and traveled smugly over the sky, knowing where it was going, and made Inga's shadow drag along behind her. On the distant sea, a little village of birds floated along, following the sun. They, too, knew where they were going.

"*Mormor! Mormor!*" Inga cried. "Grandmother!"

Nothing but the sea.

An awful thought passed over her now, like a cold shiver when the sun hides behind a cloud. She stopped. Could it be that Grandmother was now a ghost? In the old stories people liked to tell there often were ghosts.

Ghosts might be people who had died and who came back to tell their families secret prophecies or to warn them of danger.

She had not found a single footprint of Grandmother's, an image she knew well and certainly could tell from a hundred footprints on the shore, if there had been any besides her own. Could it be that Grandmother had never wavered once above the tide line to pick a berry or search a bird's nest? In all the distance that Inga had walked, would she not have found one footprint, at least?

Or was it possible she herself was a ghost? Inga pondered this. "But I make footprints now," she mumbled. Ghosts never left footprints. True, in the old stories, ghosts often looked like anyone else. You might talk to a ghost and have no idea it was not a living person – except that when you looked away for an instant the ghost disappeared.

"When Grandmother comes I will see if she leaves footprints," Inga whispered. A large flat stone came in sight, and Inga sat down to rest. She shivered, although the day was warming at last. She felt the dampness of her cloak, but as she drew out the cloak pin to dry the garment in the wind, she was startled. This was not her cloak! It was *Grandmother's!* That rich brown thread was dyed from nuts Grandmother had gathered. Inga knew that yellow thread, too. Inga had dyed it that colour herself from boiled flowers and spun that thread. This was Grandmother's cloak. And, yes, this was Grandmother's cloak pin in the palm of her hand – the pin with the ring at the top! Inga rubbed the smooth brass as if she were clasping Grandmother's hand.

Inga gazed out at the sea. She had spent the whole day yesterday without noticing this cloak. Or had Grandmother's ghost come in the night and changed cloaks with her, giving her this long, thick garment to keep her warm? Did she want to let her granddaughter know she was nearby in some mysterious way? Ghosts were known to protect the living.

Inga drew in an aching breath. Somehow she *knew* it now. Or had she always suspected, in her deepest heart, that Grandmother would never have left her alone on the shore? *Grandmother was never coming again to leave her footprints above the tide.*

Inga stood up on the flat rock. She grasped the cloak pin tightly in her hand but held the cloak by its corners to let the wind lift and sway the beautiful, richly hued cloth in the sunlight.

"Grandmother," she whispered, "stay near me now."

Chapter Two

Ship Fittings

Newfoundland

The next morning Inga wrapped Grandmother's cloak around her and fastened the brass pin. By afternoon the wind changed and the day turned cold. Her head down, Inga plodded into the wind. Every day, so far, the wind had come from one direction. By her best guess, the others who had survived the wreck would have come ashore in the same direction this wind now blew.

"I will find them," Inga vowed. She went on. At times she felt so weak she could go no farther. Then she saw berries up a slope and climbed toward them. She knew who had guided her to these berries. "Thank you, Grandmother," she whispered.

Her knees folded under her as she sank onto the grass. She crammed one berry after another into her mouth. Beside her, small grey birds watched from a bush, tottering in the breeze. Their sparkly dark eyes seemed to say, "You are an intruder."

She told them, "I must eat, too. I did not mean to be here alone and lost."

Her glance wandered beyond the little grey birds to the rise at the edge of the gnarled woods. Swarms of birds whirled and cried over the ridge. In her imagination she could already taste the rich yolk of a bird's egg.

She had warned herself never to go so far as the gloomy wood. The *skraelings* – the wild people – must live there, she decided. She remembered what her neighbours in Greenland said about these savage, cruel people. In her mind, the *skraelings* looked not like people at all but like ferocious bears standing on human-like legs. They were Bear People.

Like trolls, the Bear People belonged to the storm-distorted woods. Inga never liked forests, and fortunately there were few in Greenland. Elf-Maidens lived there: beautiful but devious sorceresses.

Grandmother had often told the story of how, as a child in Norway, she had met an Elf-Maiden. Foolishly, she had set out to climb over the mountain pass to her grandparents' farm, although she was far too young to make the journey alone. She heard something stir the brush – birds plucking berries? – and when she peered closer she saw what, at first glimpse, she took for the shadow of antlers. Then the creature turned back toward the little wanderer. An extraordinary woman faced her, with streaming blond hair and a beautiful, sleek body tangled in flowers and vines. It was an Elf-Maiden! She stared at the little girl with her peculiar eyes, and, most alarming of all, this particular Elf-Maiden bore a monstrous pair of antlers protruding from her golden hair. In moments the magical being disappeared into the brush, for such supernatural creatures are wary of humans. Many years later, Grandmother had shuddered in telling the story.

Inga thought of how Arne Stefansson, the expedition's captain, had scorned these old notions. People were not supposed to believe in such things any more: fortune tellers, trolls, elf-people, ghosts. Yet Inga could tell by the way people told stories at the winter fireside that, in their deepest hearts, they knew these things could still be there.

Trolls and *skraelings* belonged to shadows and grim woods, to mountaintops, caves and wild glens. Everyone knew the Bear People were supernatural beings, too. But, maybe, she could go safely as far as that stony ridge where the birds hovered over nests of fresh eggs.

Even from this distance, she could hear the squabbling birds. Her fear and her hunger warred against each other. "If I creep slowly enough," she murmured. Before she was aware of it, she was crossing the rough, hummocked ground. Sod hid lumps of rock. She stumbled but went on. Pools dotted the surface, and cruel breezes shook visions of the sky on the water. Fluffy birds' down tumbled in the grass, and the bewitched feathers beckoned her to come closer, closer.

Her mind travelled back to the farm where she would slip a hand into a warm goose nest and add the eggs she found there to her basket. Grandmother was always pleased to see how many eggs she had gathered. At last, Inga reached the bank. Her eyes fastened on the panicked birds as she climbed up the ridge. Shrill alarms rang in the air. Scrambling higher, she glimpsed the shore behind her and the distant blue inlets. For an instant she recognized places she had passed, but her hunger drove her thoughts back to food ahead.

With birds diving above her, Inga hid under Grand-mother's cloak. Quickly, she stole an egg first from one nest and then another, enveloped in screaming warnings. Frantic birds flew so close she felt the breath of their wings. By the time she reached an enormous boulder to hide behind, the birds considered her driven off, and returned to their nests. Inga hid in the boulder's shadow and broke one fragile shell after another, letting the white drip first into her mouth, and then the rich, yellow yolk. She kept three large eggs for later.

Longingly she looked back over the land at the sea and yearned now to soak her sore feet in the soft waves. As she watched the distant blue touched with white foam, she realized suddenly how blindly she had crossed the land to the ridge. She must never be so careless again, no matter how hungry she might be. From her rocky perch she saw no Bear People. No wolves. No ghosts or trolls. She was safe, for now. Squinting in the wind, she searched the coast. She saw no mast or prow on the beach, no boat upended on a sandbar. No one.

She began to clamber down. Near the foot of the bank she discovered signs of another living being. Abundant feathers and down lay strewn about. She saw bloody smears on the rocks, but the blood was not fresh. These signs she recognized. They told the story of a predator raiding the birds' nests on the ridge, not for eggs but for fledglings. An eagle, a hawk? Then in the thick mud she saw a familiar print: wolves! She shivered and scrambled over the last few rocks.

The scattered black feathers at the very bottom she also knew well. She picked up a glossy feather, watching how the light caught the blue gleam in its blackness.

"*Ravn*," she whispered. Ravens followed wolves or even led them to their prey, hoping to share some of their kill. One had come too close. Beside a briar, she found a dead raven, matted with blood, its feet curled up. Something else rustled under the rocks, too. Crouching, she peered into a crevice in the split rock and saw something alive and as dark as the shadow itself. Another raven. The bird made a weak but threatening noise.

"*Ravn*," she said to the hiding bird, "the wolf is gone. Fly home." With a sigh, Inga longed to be a raven and fly – fly home – over the rocking blue water. She laid her precious eggs in the grass and crawled as near as she could to the raven's hiding place. This was a young raven, perhaps, not a new fledgling but a young bird. The dead bird's offspring? When he opened his beak to warn her away, the inside of his mouth showed pink, and this she knew to be the sign of a young raven. The raven snapped up grass, threw it this way and that. He hurled a pebble, shook his head and uttered a deep, rasping warning.

"*Ravn*, you must try harder if you hope to scare me," Inga replied.

The bird hammered at the rock over his head. Finally his energy gave out. He stopped, breathed deeply and lowered his head.

"Are you hurt, little one?" Inga asked. She thought about the way they caught a goose back at the farm. To avoid the pinching bill, you had to grasp the long neck just below the head and wrap an arm around the folded wings. Mind the wings, Grandmother always said. A goose could whack hard with the bony joints of its wings.

Inga studied the raven. His beak was thick, not sharp but strong. Like geese, the raven had no teeth. Yet many times she had seen ravens tear apart fish they had caught. The feet had sharp claws, too. Grandmother could grab a goose by the bill and hold it shut, but she warned that the bill must be held tightly or the goose would pinch your fingers. Inga did not want to try holding the raven's strong beak. No, she had to find a way to come up behind him. First, he must be prodded from his hiding place.

Though the raven now huddled quietly, his beak resting on the ground, Inga took no chances. With a twig, she gently poked the bird out of the hole. His dark eyes flashed, and he rasped a menacing threat. But he had no strength left to fight her off. He had a gash on the joint of his wing. A bloody spot showed on his back. She held up one of her cache of eggs to his beak, but the young raven was too weak to eat. She broke open the egg and held out the juicy innards. When he still refused to eat, she drank this nourishment herself, not wanting to waste it.

Inga wrapped the raven in her cloak, gathered the remaining eggs and headed toward the shore. After tenderly bathing the raven's wounds in the healing sea water, she found some mussels and cut the meat into small bits with a broken shell. She offered them to the thick beak of the raven. The bird blinked. She chewed a piece until it was even softer and tried again. After a moment the raven nibbled a morsel. Then she offered one piece after another.

As day ended, Inga stopped by a rocky bank. She gathered nearby rushes and stalks and reeds and wove them together to make a long, stiff mat, like the fences people at home made to pen animals. Under this mat, Inga and the raven huddled as night fell. Wrapped in Grandmother's cloak, they rested out of the wind. Inga fell to sleep, hoping the raven would live through the night. It was good to have something beside her, wiggling and sniffing and mumbling.

When she opened her eyes with the morning light, the raven was there – and alive. He lifted his head and burbled at her softly. They shared the two remaining eggs, and this time the raven readily accepted her gifts. The mat had helped keep them warm and dry. Promptly Inga braided two loops on the sides of the mat. She slipped her arms through the loops to hold the mat over her back. Together Inga and the raven continued along the lonely coast, searching for whatever they could find to sustain them.

After three days, the raven was strong enough to ride on Inga's shoulder. She wove a small net and attached it to a stick. With this she captured tiny fish feeding by the rocks. The fish were small but made a tasty, salty bite. These the raven ate with a low, happy sound, something like a purring cat, Inga thought. His wing appeared to be sore but not broken. Now well fed, his cuts washed repeatedly, the raven held his head higher and observed the world around them. He was not strong enough to fly, but he barked a short warning call when a rabbit bolted over the grass or a fox fled into the bush. The raven was an excellent guard.

They saw no people, not a Norseman nor one of the Bear People. As far as the latter were concerned she was thankful. She felt safer with the raven, whatever dangers lay near.

Two more days passed. By then, the raven gripped Inga's shoulder more firmly and held himself upright. When he wanted to sleep, the raven closed his eyes and lowered his beak, clinging fast to his shoulder perch.

Twilight yellowed the western sky one day as they patrolled the beach, digging shellfish out of the mud. The raven saw something ahead. He let out a single, harsh warning. Inga stopped. "I see it, little one," she whispered. There were dark specks on the shore. She waited for the specks to move. They remained motionless, so they were not birds. Were they seals? Boats? Could they be *skraelings*?

She hid behind a rock. Surely she would see some small movement if they were Bear People. The specks did not move, no matter how long she waited. Finally, she walked closer, and the raven stretched himself tall on her shoulder, his eyes staring ahead.

The first object they found rested above the high water mark of the tide. Inga recognized it: a leather purse, the kind her people used for carrying small objects. She turned the water-stained purse over, examining its design. It contained coins, a broken needle thrust through a small piece of red cloth, a few nuts, a pair of scissors, and a small whetstone. The needle told her that this purse must have belonged to one of the women from the ship. She added to the purse other small objects she found as she walked solemnly among the ruined fragments. Finally she looped the purse strings around her neck and walked on. The raven hopped down to the sand and strode beside her, poking at wooden scraps and flinging some aside.

Half-buried wooden fragments stared from the sand and pebbles, wood that had been hewn or carved. A smooth plank peered from a clump of seaweed. There – there was the curved stave from a barrel, and over there, a round wooden circle, the bottom of a wooden tub. These were all things carried on a ship.

Brashly the raven let out a warning, "Gkkk! Gkkk! Gkkk!" Inga whirled around. What the raven saw in the relentlessly breaking waves, she saw, too: a massive, dark timber. The mast of a great ship. She stared at this looming shadow in the waves, as if it truly had come from the world of ghosts.

Then, Inga walked ahead to the big fragments of wreckage farther on. Some were curved planks fitted with neatly spaced rivets; others were wound with twists of rope. She picked up two smaller, sculpted pieces. These she recognized. They were carved fittings of the kind that men create to build a ship, one of a soft cone shape with a stem like a mushroom, the other a cylinder with stems on each end. When she was a little child, she had watched her grandfather carve fittings like these. Yes, this must be Arne Stefansson's ship – *her* ship.

Inga held the ship fittings close, and searched further. There were shreds of sail, more barrels and tubs, fragments of wood pierced by nails. She and the raven searched in ever-widening circles – until they saw no more remnants of the wreck. Ahead stretched lonely sand and grass.

There were no human footprints leading to the small pond beyond the bank where a person might go for drinking water. There were no prints leading to the shelter of bushes, no charred fragments of a fire someone had lighted with a strike-a-light kept safe in a purse.

At last, worn to despair, Inga sat on the bank and watched the red sun paint the empty sea. The nightmare had been real. Once more, in her memory, she heard the roar of the storm, the slap of the sea against the small boat as she and Grandmother rocked over the waves. Now far, far out on the horizon the last light of the sun touched the water, making a path, flaming as though it would burn to ash.

Once more her tears would not be refused. This time she cried hard, bitter tears. How long she sat there, she could not have said. Finally, it was the raven poking at her shoulder who tugged her out of this cloud of grief. The raven murmured friendly sounds to her and nibbled her fingers when she reached up to pet him. Her tears stopped. She realized something important. At least, with the raven, she was not alone. And she knew who had sent him to her from the land of the spirits.

"Thank you, Grandmother," she whispered again. To the bird she said, "Yes, you are hungry, little one. Come, we will find something to fill your stomach."

She had overlooked the ship fittings that lay in her lap, and, as she stood, they tumbled down the bank, forgotten, into the soft sand.

Chapter Three

The Birch Basket

Newfoundland

One morning tendrils of mist roamed the ground. A hazy sun touched the mist with mystery and stirred the wispy fragments. Unseen seabirds cried mournfully. Inga huddled under her mat, and the raven nestled beside her. One tumbling wisp she saw resembled a bear while another looked like a woman searching for a lamb that frolicked nearby. The morning was haunted.

Inga fumbled in the leather purse she had found at the wreck. She brought out three eggs she had gathered before dark. One she cracked and held to the raven's beak. He ate hungrily. Another egg she ate herself. The third they shared between them. The raven compelled her to begin and close the day searching for food: eggs, shellfish, minnows, berries, seeds. Because the raven ate, she ate.

"You are healing well, little one," she said, petting his head feathers. The raven could already flap his wings and glide onto a nearby rock or bush and then drift back to her. Yet he was not ready to fly away.

Inga knew several of the raven's calls now, the ones that meant "thank you" and "I'm hungry," "be careful," and "I like you." Now he said, "I am still hungry."

"Yes," she whispered, "but let me rest a little longer."

At every decision she had to face, she talked to the raven. Should they walk in this direction or that? From which rock should they fish? Was that shadow dangerous? The raven always had something to babble or croak or mutter.

"I will get up soon," she promised. Inga was sure they were talking – maybe not the way people talk to each other but in some way. She hoped when he was stronger the raven would stay with her because they were friends now.

Grandmother's cloak was cozy, and she did not want to get up. Her feet were sore. Her bones ached from walking and from crouching under the mat. She fell back to sleep. In her dreams she heard the fire spitting in the centre of the room at the Greenland farm. She smelled something in a pot hung over the flames and brilliant coals. Whatever was in the pot bubbled. Somewhere nearby a dog slept, and she could hear the dog turn in its sleep and whimper. Perhaps he dreamt of the tasty bones he would soon enjoy. Around the cooking place, drops leapt from the pot and hissed on the stones. Something delicious was almost ready to eat.

The raven pulled at her ear. Inga opened her eyes. "Yes, I know," she whispered. "I will get up." The raven made a low, rasping sound: a warning. She searched the grassy plain. The sun had yellowed the mist. She heard the sea rocking restlessly. What did the raven see?

Then Inga caught sight of something moving, out there on the grass. But the shape circled, stopped – too solid for mist. Was it a hopping rabbit? The raven murmured fitful grumblings. "Hush, little one," Inga whispered. The white thing was too small for a bear, too big for a rabbit. The thing did not move like a bird.

Soon a huge wheel of mist rolled across the grass and hid the vision. When it drifted away the white thing was gone. "Gkkk! Gkkk! Gkkk!" the raven warned, moments later. Yes, he was right. The shape had re-appeared. It seemed to beckon to her, telling her to follow. Was it a ghost? Grandmother's ghost? Inga hesitated. The ghost – if it was a ghost – turned this way and that, circled, waited.

Carefully, Inga got up on her knees. The raven gripped her shoulder as she moved. She slipped her arms through the loops of the mat; perhaps they could hide behind it and not be seen in the mist, if the white thing proved dangerous. She crept over the grass. The white shape bobbed and then stopped.

"Grandmother?" Inga whispered, as softly as she could. Surely a ghost could hear a whisper, hear even the thoughts in people's minds. The white shape moved farther on. "I am coming," Inga whispered to this vision.

With mist whirling around her, she followed. The raven rustled its wings and mumbled. "Show me the way to find our friends," Inga told the white image. Grandmother's ghost must know she was lost, and that was why she had come. Now the image headed for the bushes. Inga stumbled, creeping toward it.

The strange white image danced and chased the wisps of mist. Grandmother is happy she found me, Inga thought. All of a sudden the white shape plunged out of sight into the brush. Inga dashed forward.

"Grandmother!" she cried aloud. "Wait!" She held out her hands and pushed her way through the thick branches. With a squawk the raven fluttered away from her shoulder.

The white shape stood so close she could touch it. But when the shape spun around, a face stared at Inga – but not Grandmother's face! A little girl, a horrified girl, with a round shiny face and frightened brown eyes, glared at her. The white fur of a bearskin hung over her shoulders.

Inga screamed, frozen in terror: surrounding them both stood a ring of strangers! They, too, shrank back, as alarmed at the sight of her as she was of them. Fear distorted their slender dark eyes, their rounded faces framed by long dark hair. Could they be ghosts? Did ghosts dress in animal skins ornamented with shells and fur and bone?

To Inga's frantic mind, the strangers all had the same, unfamiliar, alien face. A man with a whale tooth hanging around his neck strode forward. He stared at her in astonishment. Then he shook his wooden club, pointed at her and barked harsh, unintelligible words. Others shouted, their words mounting like a storm of strange, hard sounds. The man with the whale tooth gestured toward the shore, and a few of his companions charged off through the brush.

The whale tooth man gripped Inga's arm. He was strong and dragged her into the circle of strangers. Did he mean to kill her? Stumbling on something on the ground, she saw a dead rabbit on the grass, its blood oozing onto the earth. The voices were demanding, accusing, exclaiming, and to her every sound was meaningless.

Was the little girl in the white bearskin an Elf-Maiden, Inga wondered, come from the Norsemen's land to lure wanderers into danger? A dog pushed forward, sniffing at her. The dog growled, and a woman with shining eyes and long hair grabbed the animal by the scruff and spoke sharply to him. She pushed the dog toward a boy who sat on a rock watching Inga with a gaping mouth. Mysteriously, the strangers fell silent and stared at Inga. Only a few whispers, like whispers of sails in the wind, passed among them.

Suddenly, Inga's brain, which had been paralyzed with fear, worked out the puzzle. She saw their dark hair and eyes, the angular cheekbones, the bearskins and fur, the ivory and stone weapons. These were the Bear People! The terrible *skraelings* had captured her!

The woman with shining eyes spoke to the others in short, rough sounds. Over her skin clothing she wore a necklace of shells. Was she a sorceress? Her words sounded like the weirding words of a spell. Inga felt her own head spin, and she began to be a wild stalk blown by the wind – this way, that way.

Then, from somewhere, a dark smudge rushed toward her. The circle of *skraelings* stumbled back. With a loud croak, the raven landed on Inga's shoulder. From that perch he showered the strangers with threatening words and bristled his head and neck feathers. Their eyes wide with wonder, the Bear People stood stunned. The bird plucked leaves from Inga's braids and tossed them about. He grasped a sprig of berries caught in the mat and, holding the cluster in one claw, he pulled each berry free with his beak and heaved it toward the Bear People.

The barking dog leapt forward. The raven fluttered up then swooped and nipped the dog's tail. Pitifully the dog howled. Twice more, the raven plunged and nipped. The dog wailed, skittering behind the boy on the rock.

"*Ravn!*" Inga commanded. The raven flew instantly to her outstretched arm. He climbed up to her shoulder and sat, mumbling dark warnings.

A remarkable thing happened. The boy on the rock rose and stepped toward her. He was taller than Inga and wore a garment trimmed with feathers and shells. The boy stared at the raven – and began to laugh!

The raven gave a triumphant croak and flapped his wings. He lifted his beak, proud and boastful. The boy laughed all the harder and held out a stick with a morsel of fish bait tied at its end. The bird leapt to the stick, hung upside-down from it, pulled up the bait and gulped it down. The boy cried out with delight. The man with the whale tooth loudly scolded him, his face a deep frown.

At that instant, Inga felt herself spinning, falling, as if from a high precipice. Everything turned to darkness. She sank to the ground.

When Inga opened her eyes again, the raven stood on the grass beside her, pulling at the hair under her cap. She gasped for breath, at first unable to move. At last, she found her strength and sat upright. They were alone again. In the distance she saw the scrubby hedge she had pushed through, following the girl with the white bearskin. In the other direction was the rock where the laughing boy had sat. The bare rock cast a shadow over the ground. In the rough grass, tufts of the dog's fur tumbled. That was all. There was no sound but the babble of the nearby waves.

The Bear People were gone. But there, almost at her feet, sat a birch basket, evidently left for her. The raven strutted to this basket and promptly plucked something from it with a gulp. In the basket Inga found berries, fragments of fish and meat. Or were these bewitched things, not berries and meat at all? Once again she searched in every direction for some sign of the Bear People. She saw nothing.

Exhausted from this terrifying meeting, she sat on the rock. The raven hopped to her knee, and together they hungrily shared the food the Bear People had left her before those mysterious beings disappeared.

The fire seeketh   who with frozen feet
hath come from the cold beyond.
Food and dry clothes   the stranger needeth
over the hills who hath roamed.

Hávamál (The Sayings of Har)

Part 2

Nearing, they saw three hide-covered boats, with three men
hiding under each. They succeeded in capturing all except one
and killed the other eight then returned to the shore.

Suddenly they were struck with a mysterious sleep...
then a voice called to them, and they wakened.
"Wake up, Thorwald, and all your men," the voice told them.
"If you wish to save yourselves...return to your ship and
depart from this land as quickly as you are able."

The Greenlanders' Saga

Chapter Four

A Spindle Whorl

Newfoundland

For days, a heartless wind blew beneath a dreary sky. The raven shook his feathers time and again, insistent on neatly arranging his plumage. He grumbled, clinging to Inga's shoulder as she trudged through the brush. Anxiously, she hid from the Bear People. She stopped sharing her thoughts with the bird, fearing that even a single word might be heard by one of these strange people lurking in the bush or behind a boulder. Why had the Bear People not captured her? Was she too unimportant? Were they following her, hoping she would lead them to a camp full of Norsemen they could attack?

Once she came across a man's footprint in the sand. This reminded her to keep to the grass where her own trail would be harder to find. Moments later, as Inga climbed the slope away from the sea, the raven found something by one of her stack of stones: a flat slab of wood and on it several small fish, berries and a piece of rabbit meat. Inga quickly searched the land circling that spot but saw no one. Who could have left this food? A ghost? She was too hungry to wonder long.

The next day she was not as hungry when, again, she found more food and with it, this time, a gift: a ring of cut hide, decorated with feathers. She slipped this around her wrist, and the raven croaked pertly.

"Hush!" Inga warned.

Another time, although she thought that by then they had walked far away from the Bear People, the raven suddenly croaked and Inga looked up to catch a glimpse of someone's head above a patch of briars. The long, thick loose hair, black as night, fluttered in the wind as the vision passed out of sight. Was it the woman with the shining eyes who had grabbed the growling dog? Or was it the laughing boy who had played with the raven? Perhaps, it was someone she had never met, someone dangerous. After hiding until the sky began to give way to night, Inga and the raven went on farther until they were sure they had seen no sign of the Bear People for some time, nor any sign of a Norseman, for that matter.

The next day, while lightning flashed silently over the horizon of the sea, Inga glimpsed a band of men from the Bear People making their way down to the shore. The man with the whale tooth around his neck led the file of men and pointed toward the sea. Concealed behind a sweeping bank of sea roses, fragrant with rich pink blossoms, Inga watched. She followed, crawling from one hiding place to another.

The men walked as people do when they know the land well. She could not understand their words, but she hoped somehow to guess their plans. The raven stretched his wings lazily and leapt up to the tip of a bush. From there his keen eyes watched all that happened. Inga could make out the Bear People's knives, spears, bows and arrows. For an instant she thought she heard something behind her, as well. Was someone else following her? Or was someone following these men? While she crouched and listened, she knew the raven saw everything for her. He muttered an uneasy warning.

The men came to a spot Inga knew only too well: the rocky inlet where the Norse ship lay wrecked. Here the men stopped. This is what the Whale Tooth man sought, the secret of her strange appearance in their land. A few men were sent away, evidently to search in each direction. After an energetic exchange of words, the others searched the shore. They plucked wooden fragments from the sand and studied them, talking together. Inga hid as still as a stone.

The raven fluttered from her shoulder and landed on the shore, among a cluster of ravens waddling on the wet sand. "*Ravn!*" she whispered. But he paid no attention. The raven foraged with the other birds within sight of the men who gave them not the smallest glance. Certainly her raven looked no different from the other ravens. Like the others, he poked tiny holes in the sand and found crabs. He turned over clam shells and pried them open with his beak. But all the while, he watched.

The sun had already moved low in the west by the time the men who had been sent scouting returned. Their companions listened to their report, and she knew what they must have said: they had found no sign of the Norsemen. The Bear People knew now that she was alone, save for a strange raven. Would these men hunt her like a lame deer and slay her, since there was no revenge to be feared? Could she flee so far that they could not find her? The raven soared to her side again, and soon the men climbed through the brush and out of sight. They did not take her fears with them.

The land grew dark and the wind was cold. Inga, with the raven beside her, huddled under the mat behind the shelter of a rock. She had scarcely closed her eyes before she reached the world where dreams dwell and where, she hoped, Grandmother would be waiting to guide her.

In the morning a light rain fell. The sky seemed full of tears. Yet the raven nibbled at her ear, and Inga stirred herself. She saw that the birch basket was full again with bits of fish, meat and fruit. And another special gift.

"It's a necklace," she told the raven who helped himself to a small fish. The loop of hide was decorated with shells, each a different delicate hue of sunrises and sunsets, sand and sea, with a larger round shell in the middle. A few white bits of down were tied between the shells. The misty rain chafed her cheek, while below the bank the incoming tide simmered with foam. Its nervous fingers searched for land.

Inga dropped the necklace over her head and her long, fair braids. Eagerly, she helped the raven gobble the food but still felt hungry and alone when the basket was empty. Slowly the dim, rising sun relieved the gloom. Inga studied the gift of the necklace and grasped the big centre shell. This shell felt rough in her hands.

"Ah, it's a stone," she whispered, looking more closely. Not a shell at all. Then her mouth fell open in an unspoken cry. She held the stone in her palm, and her eyes filled with wonder. This was a stone she knew well, round and flattened with a large hole drilled in the middle. This was the flywheel of a spindle, such a stone as she had seen many, many times when spinning yarn. Stones like these also weighed down the threads on Grandmother's tall loom from which they hung just above the floor. This was a Norse spindle whorl! Inga felt her heart skip for joy! She stumbled down to the shore, blind to anything else in the world.

She thought for a moment. The Bear People had been dressed in hides and fur, even in summer. None of their garments, as far as she had noticed, was of woven cloth, yet here was a spindle whorl. Who could have made it but a Norse person?

No ghost would have left her a necklace, nor would a Norseman have crafted one with a spindle whorl. Her benefactor, hers and the raven's, must be one of the Bear People. Whoever it was had found the spindle whorl somewhere and, she hoped, could take her back to that place. Perhaps that person could lead her down the path to her home.

She grasped the stone in her shivering hands and held it close to her heart. Now she had hope.

Chapter Five

The Wooden Man

Newfoundland, then Southern Labrador

Misty rain fell as Inga and the raven travelled the land. She hoped they had journeyed beyond the reach of the Bear People, although sometimes she found they had merely wandered in circles, and then she would strike off in a new direction. She was so tired she could do no more than take a breath and trudge on. Brokenhearted now, she searched for her people, scarcely noticing the earth at her feet. Her clothing was torn. A knee, bruised in a stumble, kept thumping, thumping. The gifts of food stopped. She had apparently walked beyond the reach of the unknown gift-giver. While her hunger made the struggle harder, she hoped now the Bear People would think no more about her.

Breathless, Inga reached the top of a knoll one morning, her heart heavy with sadness. Feeble sunlight lifted over the rim of the visible world. From this knoll there was nothing to be seen of the Bear People. She heard neither footsteps nor voices. She had escaped the terrible *skraelings*. There was no time for lingering, however. The raven gurgled and purred at her shoulder. "Hush," she warned gently.

Soon the far-off sea would be polished with soft hues: white, pale blue, grey. "Find a beetle or berry for yourself," she told the raven. "There is no time to stop." Yet she was comforted by his affection. She thought he was glad to be with her, too. Someday there would be a sail out on the horizon and they would see a Norse ship. She would take the raven home with her.

The horizon lay as straight as a shipbuilder's rule. Straight and empty. If only she could call out loudly enough that one of her people would hear. Suddenly her voice leapt from her body like a slippery fish jumping out of her grasp.

"It is I...Inga Sigurdsdottir!" she bellowed. "And I want to go home!"

The empty sea did not listen.

"It is I! Inga Sigurdsdottir! I want to go home!" she repeated.

The sea did not turn its face to her. The far-off waves

were mute. The old, stubborn sea refused to notice. She stood unmoving. It was the raven again who tugged her from her daze. He scouted a path, burbling for her to follow. She stumbled on over the rocky ground.

"Here is our friend, the sun, at last," she said finally. "I think now the rain will—" Suddenly a shadow blanketed her as if a chunk of sky were falling.

A terrifying cry echoed: "Chooook! Choooook! Choooook! Choooook!" Above her head she saw an awful image: two powerful talons, pale with claws and shanks adorned in white feathers. These talons loomed toward her. Inga fell to the ground, the rush of wind from the bird's immense wings brushing her back. From wincing eyes, Inga saw, just ahead, a thick, rough, stick nest, huge as a table, perched atop a boulder. Once again the bird swooped. "Chooook! Choooook! Choooook! Choooook!" it shrieked. Inga dodged the horrible talons and scrambled away from the ridge toward the sea.

She heard the raven's call: "Gkkk! Gkkk! Gkkk! Gkkk!" His challenge pierced the air. "Gkkk! Gkkk! Gkkk! Gkkk!" the raven raged. Inga knew a raven was no threat to this predator. She crawled farther, and all the while the great bird swooped. She came to a string of rocks blocking her path, but she could not turn back. Gripping the edges, she pulled herself up and crossed these boulders. The great bird screamed again. Its shadow pressed against her. She felt feathers touch her back, and then an iron finger of the talons scored her scalp, sharp as a knife. Warm blood trickled down her forehead, yet, in an instant, something made the bird veer away. Could it have been her raven?

"Kah, kah, kah, kah, kah!" the raven cried, swooping overhead.

"No," Inga shouted. "Fly, *ravn!* Fly away! This bird will kill you!" If only she could get beyond the great bird's territory, the creature would leave the raven alone. "Let him not be killed," she murmured. "Let my raven live!"

Abruptly she fell down a slope. She reached out to grasp a rock, a branch, but nothing came to her desperate fingers. She slid on loose pebbles and then rolled over and over. She felt like a beetle on its back, helpless, comical. Nothing she did with flailing arms or legs could stop her fall. The cool roughness of brush and grass touched her cheek and she reached out, but the grass only cut her grasping hands. Then she bumped against a large rock. She had found the bottom of the embankment and now heard the raven's alarm in the distance.

When she opened her eyes the raven stood on a bush in front of her. "*Ravn!*" she whispered. He was alive. A few feathers stuck out oddly, but he was alive. She held up a hand and the raven hopped to her wrist. Her own hand was mottled with blood. She touched the tender gash on her scalp and wanted to cry. Her cap dangled from a single string.

With the raven urging her on, she got to her feet. To

her relief, she found her arms and legs moved in more or less the usual way. Though aching and sore, she walked toward the shore, now not far away.

By nightfall, they had not gone far, following the tide line. Inga shivered and headed into the nearby brush. She cut branches and piled them atop her mat to make a better shelter against the night chill. They shared mussels together, and as Inga fell to sleep she heard a light-fingered rain falling. In spite of herself, she thought of the warm fire that must be at the Bear People's camp. She pulled her cloak more tightly around her and utterly refused to think of the Bear People.

By morning, Inga felt her new bruises keenly. Crawling from under the mat, she saw dark clouds skidding above the horizon. But where was the raven? Then she saw him atop a swaying bush. Stretched tall and alert, he sat with his feathers toward the wind, his head cocked to one side. Inga knew that he positioned his ear to hear a distant sound more clearly. He sat unmoving, listening. She heard a sound, too. Were the Bear People coming for her? Rapidly she drew the mat over her back and hurried away. "Come, little one!" she called him.

"Rek! Rek! Rek! Rek!" the raven exclaimed, leaping into the air.

"Yes, I hear it," Inga whispered. "Hurry!" As fast as she could, Inga scurried along the waves' edge, skirting rocks and pools of water. Silently the raven drifted ahead of her from perch to perch. When Inga threw herself onto a round rock to rest, she lifted her head to listen again. The sound they heard was neither a rustle of branches nor the rhythm of footsteps. It was a voice. The sound was faint, but she was grateful that there was but a single call. Was it only a hurt animal? It might be the voice of a little bird or a fox kit. Or was it...a human voice?

Around her the cold wind swirled, and for an instant she imagined the end of the brief summer. Snow would come. Ice would grip the earth. She would have to survive the winter on her own, make a shelter, snare rabbits, keep a fire. These thoughts fell over her like the weight of an enormous stone.

The voice cried out again.

From his perch on a tumble of stones, the raven shifted his gaze to Inga. His wild eyes watched her. The choice, the raven's eyes told her, was hers to make. Crouching, Inga made her way slowly inland toward the perplexing cry. With every step, she felt her thoughts warring: Was this the trick of the Bear People to capture her? Was it the cry of some vicious animal she had never seen? Could it be the voice of a ghost or the magic of an evil spirit or troll? Until she knew, she dared not cry out in reply.

Nearby, a swath of rocks led toward a slope. Inga stopped. The sound came from a large pile of rocks ahead: a wailing voice, small, thin.

"Go," she whispered to the raven. "See what it is."

She need not have asked. The raven was curious

enough. He drifted ahead and lighted atop the pile of rocks. He blinked at something below. But he did not appear frightened. Venturing closer, Inga glimpsed the shadow of a deep hole within the rocks. The raven's dark eyes stared at this hole, and they looked puzzled. What could be in that hole that a raven did not know?

Inga crept closer. Soon she peered down the hole, as well. Then the cry from within burst out in a frightened squeal. As Inga leaned over, a spray of pebbles caught her in the face.

"Yahh!" she cried, staggering back. At first, the voice in the hole fell silent. Moments later the creature uttered a flurry of gibberish.

"It's a troll, all right," Inga whispered to the raven. She listened as the troll spoke in fitful outbursts, some meek, some insistent. It sounded like a very small troll. From the smell of the place, the hole must have once been a fox den. Had the foxes hurt the little troll? Perhaps it was being punished. But Inga knew better than to pity a troll. Trolls were full of tricks. They could turn themselves into what looked like harmless little creatures so people would be tempted to help them. She could hear now that the sound in the hole had changed. She stepped closer, amazed. The troll was crying. Did trolls cry?

Inga peered cautiously over the edge. "*Du*, little troll. Don't be sad. I can't help you. I am just a lost girl myself. Soon a big troll will come by and save you." The little troll did not throw any more pebbles. The raven hopped closer and peered in the hole. "I think there's no danger," Inga told him. "This troll isn't big enough to—" At that moment a small object was tossed from the hole, grazing Inga's cheek. The raven poked at the small piece of wood that had landed on the ground.

Inga picked it up. The object was a tiny man, carved from a piece of wood. She sat down, confused. Was this a playing piece for a game, for the little man's face was featureless. No, it was a toy. Perhaps little trolls played with toys, too, like little children. Or could it be that the creature down the dark hole was not a troll at all? The raven was at her side as she leaned farther down the hole to have a look.

By sunset of the next day, Inga knew the Bear People's camp could not be far off. As they walked along the shore to reach the camp more swiftly, the child she had thought a troll — the little girl with the white bearskin — held Inga's hand tightly. In her other hand, the little girl gripped the tiny wooden man. There was no other way to bring the lost child back to her people but to lead the little girl herself.

Painfully, Inga wished there were someone to lead her back to the Norse people. She could not help glancing out on the horizon where she hoped with all her heart to see the sail of a ship. The sea was lonely.

The Bearskin Girl was tired and hungry. Inga felt the same, so sore that she wanted to cry. Her legs were stiff. Ahead of them, the raven drifted from bush to rock to briar. The bird looked back to be sure they were both following. Suddenly he rose up and returned to Inga's shoulder. Bearskin Girl cried out and crouched down.

"It's all right," Inga said, holding out her arm so that the raven glided down and began sidling down to her elbow. "He won't hurt you." Bearskin Girl peeked out from behind her splayed hand. Inga knew the child could not understand her Norse words. She reached for a berry and held it out for the raven. He plucked it up happily with a chortle. Inga placed a berry in the child's palm and held the hand up in the air. Bearskin Girl watched, wide-eyed.

"Closer," Inga said, gesturing. The raven gobbled up the berry. Bearskin Girl giggled. As if laughing, too, the raven squawked and glided over to a tall plant. Bearskin Girl must know that the bird was leading her home, Inga thought. She wondered if the raven could lead the child all by himself.

The child skipped after him as he drifted from perch to perch. At each stop, he looked back at Inga. "Aren't you coming, too?" the raven seemed to say with his eyes.

Inga and the child walked on. As children will, the girl tired of carrying her toy, and so Inga carried the little wooden man for her. At last, they heard voices calling in the distance as the sky began darkening, voices calling as people do when searching for someone lost: the same words over and over.

All the fears of the Bear People she had been taught swept over her like a crawling spider sneaking over her skin. Inga could go no farther. The child could follow the voices now, she thought. She herself must run. *She must run!*

Someone climbed into the open from a bank ahead of them: the boy who had laughed at the raven. Behind him, a dog stuck out his head for a look, but the animal had learned to be wary of the black bird. The boy stood, watching Inga and the child and the chittering raven. Slowly he took a step toward them, then two, three. Again he stopped, watched. Inga saw something now. Around his neck a whimsical necklace hung: a ring of hide decorated with feathers and shells and seedpods, not unlike the necklace she wore herself. He smiled. This Laughing Friend boy was the gift-giver. He had given her the spindle whorl necklace, a token of the world she had lost. He waved at them and called out words that, although she could not understand them, sounded happy to her ears.

Suddenly another figure rushed out of the gathering darkness: the woman with the shining eyes. She, too, stopped and stared. The cry of the child at seeing her was like a screeching seabird. The little Bearskin Girl dashed ahead toward her, and Inga knew the woman must be her mother. The woman lifted the child into her arms, murmuring gentle words and crying with joy. The child squirmed in her embrace and pointed at Inga, babbling quickly. The woman stared. The child's words had turned her mother's glance to marvel and alertness.

Voices in the distance became running figures and each, emerging from the dusk, stopped with astonishment, seeing a Norse girl standing there. Someone called out a warning, but the child's mother stopped them all with a cry and an outstretched hand. She motioned to her little girl and to Inga and explained something to her hearers in earnest words. Then she turned and held out her hand to Inga.

From somewhere the raven swooped down before Inga, uttering a loud command. He waited for her, too. The raven hopped ahead and then looked back. "Are you coming?" his eyes and his dark, curved beak seemed to ask her again.

Inga stared searchingly at the raven. "Ahh," she whispered, thunderstruck. Yes, he was leading her. Surely, he had been leading her all along, since the very day she had found him. Why hadn't she understood before? Grandmother had sent this raven to lead her, yes, to lead her toward these strange people.

The woman with the shining eyes spoke kind words and lifted her hand, the palm open toward Inga. Come, she seemed to say.

"Yes, Grandmother," Inga murmured to the bird, who fluttered to her shoulder. Inga reminded herself that the boy had given her the spindle whorl. That was important. He could show her the way to her people. That must be part of Grandmother's plan.

She took two steps forward. "I am coming, Grandmother," she whispered to the raven. After those two steps the next came more easily.

When they neared the Bear People's camp, at last, firelight flickered in the distance. The woman led her to a spot full of grassy hummocks. The raven stood on Inga's shoulder, bobbing his head, nibbling her ear. "Hush, little one," Inga whispered. She saw, in a clearing of flat earth, figures moving in the firelight, scurrying away as she advanced. Nearby, incoming waves splashed, a sound that mixed with the murmurs of the alarmed Bear People.

The Laughing Friend boy walked just ahead of her. When he turned back to her, his smile sparkled. For some reason he was not afraid at all.

With her rescued child dozing at her shoulder, the Shining Eyes woman spoke quickly to those gathered around and gestured from moment to moment at Inga. Others soon ventured into the firelight and glared at the strange girl. Shining Eyes motioned for Inga to sit by the fire. Then Inga started. Along the shore she saw dark mounds. Yet the raven apparently saw nothing to alarm him. "You are right, little one," she whispered. These mounds were only boats turned upside-down so their rounded hulls were silhouetted in the glow.

Inga's feet were heavy. They did not want to move closer. Even if Grandmother had led her here, she could not stop fear from shimmering through her body. Shining Eyes motioned to another woman to take the sleeping child away. Shining Eyes then invited Inga to the fire again. This time Inga sat down by the soothing warmth of the campfire. Shining Eyes sat next to her, meeting each pair of frowning and inquisitive eyes around them with a defiant glare. Laughing Friend came to join them and with a charred stick drew pictures on a rock. He drew a lively picture of the raven. He was surely a craftsman, Inga thought.

After Inga had eaten, Shining Eyes led her to one of the upturned boats propped up with stones. There, sheltered beneath it, Bearskin Girl already lay sleeping on her white bearskin. The woman motioned to Inga to take a place beside the little girl and then walked away toward the fire where people had gathered, muttering to each other.

The raven dropped down beside Inga. Weary and bewildered, Inga placed her mat on the ground under the shelter of the boat, unpinned her cloak and lay down on the mat. She felt the darkness creep closer. Darkness nipped her feet and the ends of her pale braids. Darkness sniffed at her like a hungry animal.

The Bear People were unlike any people she had ever seen. It was hard to be anything but frightened. The smells in their camp were odd, and their hard, noisy speech sounded menacing. As Inga lay on her mat, she touched the hull of the overturned boat whose prow rested on a rock to shelter her and the Bearskin Girl. This boat was crafted from animal skins stretched over a frame. It was not made of smoothed wooden planks like a Norse boat. She felt its rough, tight face. Implements had been deftly used to prepare this hide. She could smell the cured skins. She looked around her into the night. Yet, surely, Inga thought, there was something sinister in this alien world.

The raven stood on the sand nearby. His thick beak and shiny eyes faced the firelight. He waited, attentive to all around him. Because of him, she felt safer. Bearskin Girl slept beside her. Of course, she was not like a Norse girl. Her hair was straight and thick and shone like a wintry stream coursing through the snow. Her clothing was of hide and fur without one bit of woven cloth. Yet Inga had to admit that Bearskin Girl seemed to be a happy child.

As Inga lay her head down again, she felt something hard against her arm: the little girl's toy man. For the first time, she studied the figurine closely. She could not help the sound of surprise that slipped from her throat. The little wooden man was dressed in a long tunic, and over his chest something remarkable was carved: a simple cross. This little wooden man was not of the Bear People. He was Norse! The carver of this toy had seen a Norseman. Again, she found reason to believe that the Bear People knew how to make contact with her people. Perhaps the Norse were not that far away. She had been given another sign of hope.

"Thank you, Grandmother," Inga whispered as she lay down to sleep.

Despite her fears, Inga slept a deep, exhausted sleep under the shelter of the skin boat. Dawn brought a yellow sun hiding behind a cloth of clouds. The raven squinted into the morning light as he waited at her side. His black eyes watched the Bear People. Inga saw now that the shadowy dwellings she had seen the night before were mere tents of fur-covered hides hung over a frame of bone and wood. These tents the people now dismantled in haste. Nor were there many people in their group. This was the site of a hunting expedition, not a settled village.

With few words everyone packed and launched the boats. The Bear People appeared anxious to depart. Soon Inga, and the raven, too, sat in a boat. Whale Tooth sat behind her, dipping his paddle in the water. Men called to each other over the water, while Whale Tooth pointed toward the direction they soon headed. They turned away from the land where Inga had come ashore in the shipwreck and travelled rapidly away from the rising sun. Fearfully, Inga saw the site of the camp fade and a new rocky coast loom toward them. How were her people to find her so far away?

Yet she needed no understanding of their words to realize why the Bear People hurried from the land they left behind. They looked back at the shore with fearful eyes. Clearly it must have been only Bearskin Girl's absence that had delayed their departure once they learned that Norsemen were near. Nevertheless, they had taken her, a Norse girl, away with them. She could not tell whether this was a sign of good fortune or the opposite.

The trip was long, and in her weariness, Inga dozed and finally slept for some time. When she woke the veiled sun was ready to set. They approached a different land, stony and hilly with abrupt cliffs and sparse clumps of dark woods. They soon reached a settlement on a small bay. From afar Inga recognized the houses of a modest-sized village. These houses reminded her of the upturned boats: dark mounds against the land. They were solid houses this time, made of turf and stone. Along the shore, more skin boats lay upturned.

People gathered to greet the arriving boats. When they saw the fair-haired Inga in Whale Tooth's boat, they started. People buzzed with amazement as the prows slipped ashore. They did not welcome their visitor. More people hastened from the houses to see what had happened. Whale Tooth jumped from the boat and called to the people, holding his palm toward Inga. He spoke, while his hearers studied Inga with curiosity.

As if taunting them, the raven jumped atop Inga's head and sputtered a string of loud notes. He flapped his wings. Despite their wary parents, several children rushed to observe this feathered character. Inga plucked up a stick floating in the tide and held it in front of her. The raven immediately glided down to the stick and hung upside-down. Inga felt lucky to have a show-off for a friend. The Bear People did not spend all their time staring at her. The raven was much better amusement.

The raven fluttered over and landed on Laughing Friend's head. He tugged a feather from the boy's hair ornament. "Yuhh!" the boy cried and tried to get the feather back, but the raven was too quick. Teasing, the bird darted above the boy's head, out of reach. Finally, he swooped back to Inga's stick, tucked his stolen feather in a claw and let out a proud squawk. He bit the feather's end and, with his beak, babbled like a happy, little thief. Laughing Friend chuckled as heartily as the little children.

The raven was her magic, Inga thought. He cast a spell over the Bear People.

Shining Eyes led her to a turf house where an old woman sat sewing by the door. The old woman's thick hair was grey and her face deeply wrinkled. The woman tried to look as if she had no idea a stranger was in the house, but she wore an expression of someone who has tasted sour fruit.

Shining Eyes' house had a dark entrance passage that led into the central room. The house was dug into the ground, and Inga knew this would keep it warmer in the winter. Stored in pits at the side were cooking pots, tools, and skins and furs. In the centre a stone cooking pot rested in the fire-making place. Yet this was far different from a Norse house. There were no bright cloths hanging from the walls to add cheerfulness and warmth. There were no fancifully carved posts or big chests with ornamented metal clasps and bands. Yet, Inga had to admit, it was a snug small house.

She remembered that the Bear People were said to have evil powers. Could that old woman by the door change herself into a bird? Maybe her powers could be used to trick the raven into finding Inga's people so the men could capture them. Inga returned the old woman's gaze with her own wary glance.

At the fireside Shining Eyes rubbed a soothing oil on Inga's cut scalp. Bearskin Girl sat beside them and watched Inga with interest. She held up her finger to the raven, who nibbled its tip so gently he caused no harm but made the child laugh.

Could these people be trolls? Inga wondered. They were strange beings for trolls. Shining Eyes gave her soup in a stone bowl, a warm, welcome broth.

Through the open entrance, Inga glimpsed people carrying packs of furs and stores of meat from the boats. Soon all the boats lay upturned on the shore. Whale Tooth entered and sat at Shining Eyes' side with Laughing Friend and little Bearskin Girl. Inga realized they were a family. They ate at the fire, talking cheerfully. They watched, amused, as Inga shared rabbit meat with the raven. The bird received this admiration with his usual noisy vanity.

Laughing Friend wore a merry, secretive expression. This time the raven burbled a friendly greeting to him. The boy held one hand behind his back, hiding something, at last showing it to the raven: a tasty bit of fish the raven snapped up at once. Laughing Friend liked to play with the raven. Could he be her friend, too? He might teach her where the spindle whorl had been found and tell her who had carved the child's wooden man.

He will lead me home, Inga thought.

Part 3

*The seeress called for the women who knew the songs
needed for chanting the rites, songs that are called Varthlokkur,
weirding songs.*

*Gudrid told her, I have no powers nor can I foretell the future,
but in Iceland, my mother taught me the songs...
yet these are things that now I cannot take part in,
because I am a Christian woman.*

*The seeress said to her that she might help the people
here by joining the rites, and she would be the better for this,
the seeress added...*

*The women formed a weirding ring around the place set for
the ceremony, and Thorbjorg, the seeress, stood in the centre
of it. Gudrid spoke the weirding songs so finely that no one
could remember having heard so beautiful a voice.*

Eirik the Red's Saga

Chapter Six

The Stone Lamp

Southern Labrador

A few months later the cloudberry blossoms and their golden fruit had disappeared. Autumn approached. On a knoll, Inga faced the sea where the rich smell of seaweed filled the breeze and something spicy-scented bloomed in the brush. With the raven on her shoulder, Inga scanned the far edge of the sea. From this spot, overlooking the Bear People's village, she often envisioned the marvellous form of a Norse ship appearing on the horizon. Today that distant place was a sharp blue in the clear, crisp weather. Once more, the horizon was empty.

She knew Uncle Knut's ship must have sailed for home by this time. It was unlikely he had heard anything of a shipwreck, especially since she alone had survived. These days she felt like a bird blown astray in a storm, landing far from home in an unknown land.

Around her neck the spindle whorl dangled from the necklace Laughing Friend had made for her. She gripped the smooth stone and held it close. Over at the clustered houses, the Bear People were busy. As soon as the seals began migrating southward, expeditions set out to hunt them. Small parties also set out northward in search of the caribou. Today Whale Tooth would lead a hunting party. Inga had quickly learned that he was an important man among the Bear People.

Little by little, these people had become less frightening. They reminded her of those she knew on farms in her own fjord back home in the eastern settlement. She had come to know Shining Eyes and Whale Tooth, playful Bearskin Girl and many others in the village, too.

There was wise Broken Smile, with his missing front tooth. A skilful fisherman, Broken Smile always laughed to see the raven prowl along a sandbar. The bird, now vigorous and healthy, deftly snatched fish from the curling water. He spotted his prey with a cheerful gurgle. Then there was Watching Eyes, the old woman who often sat at the doorway. She rarely spoke, though her eyes hid many words as she sat sewing or preparing an animal hide. Sometimes when Inga felt someone watching her, she looked up to find it was Watching Eyes' glance she had sensed falling over her like a shadow. Watching Eyes had been slow to accept this strange, fair-haired girl. Inga decided the old woman must be a grandmother or an aunt without a family, maybe a childless widow, for she went from house to house, helping one family and then another. She was the kind of person whose opinion is never asked, though Inga thought she would have much to say.

One day, Inga had approached Watching Eyes, who sat by the doorway on a damp, foggy morning. Inga had given her the mat she had made. "Please, take it," Inga had urged, hoping her gestures conveyed her thoughts. "You will be more comfortable." The woman understood nothing of this speech, Inga knew, but reluctantly, Watching Eyes had studied the mat and finally placed it on the ground to sit on. Inga wove more mats and gave them away to others. Curious eyes approved the careful, even weaving – a skill her people valued.

Inga liked the lovely Blue Shell and her husband, the spindly Cut Eye. Their two sons were long-legged fellows who excelled in all the games the boys of the village played together. Inga thought of these sons as Grasshopper and Cricket, on account of their merry behaviour. Their older sister, Silk Hair, was obviously in love with Red Shoes, a young man who tried hard to look grown-up and important. Inga thought Red Shoes felt the same about Silk Hair, but he didn't think he should show it. That might not be the grown-up thing to do.

Laughing Friend was like a brother to her. The two of them spent the days gathering berries and driftwood, drawing pictures on the stones with bits of charred wood, and catching fish along the shore. The boy was an expert at carving in stone, bone and ivory. He crafted figures of things around them: a fox, a bear, a seal, and the people of the village – a chubby child or an old man. Some of the Bear People took a small ivory figure – a bird or a fish perhaps – and fastened it to their clothing. This was to bring luck or protection, she guessed. Inga enjoyed watching Laughing Friend work. She herself wove fine nets with strings of sinew or hide, and they lowered these from rocks to catch fish. Laughing Friend whittled a sharp spear. Together they caught food for the village. Always the raven accompanied them, amusing the boy with his antics.

Whatever especially interesting shell or bone fragments or polished bits of woods they found the boy made into ornaments. Sometimes his handiwork became toys for the children. There were few among the Bear People who had not received his gifts. He was a kind boy. Surely, Inga thought, he would help her find the Norse camp. But how was she to encourage him? How could she explain her deep sorrow when she and the boy spoke impossibly different languages? Did he find the words she spoke as bizarre as she found the words of the Bear People? Once or twice she had thought of trying to learn a few words of their odd tongue. She understood this might help her find her people, and yet these were not the words of her homeland. She did not belong here. Something in her resisted the strange words. Speaking her own language showed who she was: a Norse girl. A Norse girl she must remain.

Standing up on the knoll that morning, she felt the raven pick at her cap. "Hungry again?" she said. She reached in the leather purse and brought out berries she had saved for him. The raven gobbled them up. His feet tickled as he stood in her hand. "We cannot wait for the Bear People to stumble across our friends," she told the bird. "Somehow we must persuade them to look for our people." Every day she hoped someone would dash into the village, bursting with news of strange sights: tall, pale people in odd clothing or a square-sailed ship that sped by like the wind. But nothing like this scene had taken place.

Laughing Friend approached and bound up the knoll to join her. He chimed a happy greeting. It would be hard not to trust Laughing Friend. Perhaps she could learn just a few of his words. She decided to make his familiar greeting her first word. She tried to imitate its peculiar sounds. The boy started. She repeated her effort twice. Then Laughing Friend chuckled. He repeated the greeting, a phrase that felt jagged in her mouth. She tried repeating it. This time he smiled, although half-heartedly.

The boy made a face at the raven and held out his hand. There was a minnow.

"Oh," Inga said to the raven, "you are lucky in your friends." The bird hopped to his hand and downed the treat with a squawk. Laughing Friend then uttered his strange, energetic words and gestured toward the west. She noticed that he carried a berry basket and knew then what he had in mind. "Berries," she said with a smile to show her readiness. She fell in beside him as he led the way. The raven followed, gliding from bush to bush, and sometimes called to other ravens he could hear.

At long last they came to a rise of land, skirting a dense patch of stunted trees. Overhead, hawks circled, searching for mice and rabbits. The boy shouted and whistled to them. Cleverly, the raven imitated his whistle. The hawks paid no attention to either of them. Soon a rocky promontory came in sight. "This must be a fine berrying place," Inga said, "to walk so far." Abruptly, Laughing Friend charged up the slope that led to a precipitous cliff above a boisterous sea. Inga ran after him while the raven flapped his wings overhead in the fresh, salty air.

When they reached the top of the slope, she saw a hidden, shadowy slope tucked under the other side. There, cloudberries were still abundant. The golden orange of the fruit shone like firelight. The boy popped a berry in his mouth. He laughed. This treat was hard to resist, and they both sampled the delicious fruit. When their basket reached the halfway mark, Laughing Friend touched her arm. "What is it?" she asked. He nodded toward the water, squinting in the sunshine. A boat approached in the distance. Inga caught her breath. The boy smiled. He was not worried.

"Boat?" Inga said brightly, hoping this might be a useful new word he could teach her. "Boat?" she repeated. He did not take her hint, however. She soon saw that the craft was one of the sort used by the Bear People. Two men made good speed over the water. Whoever they were, they knew the waters well, for they veered widely around rocks almost hidden beneath the surface.

The boy pointed farther to a spot next to a hedge of briars. There the cloudberries were luscious, ripening late in the lack of full sunshine. He led the way. Cloudberries. That should be an easy word to learn, she thought. She pointed to the gold-orange clusters at their feet and looked expectantly at him. This time Laughing Friend's face brightened. He nodded and spoke the word slowly twice. Encouraged, she repeated it carefully, with success this time, for he smiled his full approval. She thought of all the fun they would have learning new words together. But it must not be too fun, she reminded herself. These words were only to help her find a Norse encampment. Again she whispered the new word to herself. Merrily, they returned to plucking the irresistible fruit.

"Gkkk! Gkkk! Gkkk! Gkkk! Gkkk!" the raven sputtered. He shook his head feathers firmly. She looked around but there was nothing to support his alarm.

"If you're hungry, eat some berries," Inga told him. She popped a berry in her mouth and pronounced her new word again to Laughing Friend. He grinned and led her onward through the berry patch. The raven swooped ahead, blocking their path. He sputtered impatiently. The boy offered him berries in his open palm. The raven pulled his beak aside. He hopped farther away, flapping his wings and shaking his feathers.

"Stop it!" Inga ordered when the bird began diving at them and making low, rasping sounds. Then Inga studied him closely. "Wait," she whispered to the boy. If only she knew the words to explain! "The raven is speaking to us. We should go back, he says." She pointed in the direction of the village.

Laughing Friend tilted his head, not understanding. He walked ahead and plucked a fat berry, dropping it in his mouth. "Mmm," he said. The raven shrieked and rose in the air. He swooped over the briar hedge and disappeared.

Inga gripped the boy's shoulder. "Shh," she warned. They both fell silent, for now she heard something rustling. The sound seemed to come from thick grass beyond the berry patch. The raven leapt high into the air then dived out of sight. Inga and Laughing Friend crouched low. They could see the raven rising and swooping beyond the hedge. He cackled wildly and flapped his wings. Then a furry paw rose from the grass and swiped at the noisy raven.

"Naagh!" the boy gasped. The basket of berries somersaulted to the ground. The two friends looked at each other, and she knew that in his own language he spoke a word whose meaning was obvious: bear! They peered through the brush and saw first one and then two bear cubs tumbling in the grass, pawing at the taunting raven. Cubs meant a mother bear was nearby, ready to protect them. No bear was more dangerous. Laughing Friend searched and found a round stone. This he held up, ready to fight off an attack. But while the raven busied the cubs with his frantic calls and diving, they were able to crawl away. They kept well out of sight of the cubs, hiding behind any rock or brush they came across. They knew the cubs' whining and hooting were sure to bring their mother running.

As she crept farther and farther, Inga still heard the raven's frenzied calls. She longed to call the raven back. The raven had saved them, but would his brave tricks mean his death? Then they heard the raven squawk. The boy tugged her down and gripped his stone tightly. On a slippery stretch of mud, Laughing Friend grasped her arm to keep her from sliding down a bank. Up the slope a shadow loomed, the massive form of the mother bear bounding toward her crying cubs. Her deep, angry growl made the two friends shiver.

Inga rose to her knees, ready to call out a warning to the raven, but the boy held his hand over her mouth. They did not move until the bear was out of sight. Laughing Friend then gripped her hand and they hurried away. When they came to open ground, he stopped. She knew exactly what had caught his attention. The sounds of the raven had ceased.

They raced on to the village. Laughing Friend shouted a warning as they came in sight. Men ran for their weapons. Dogs barked. Mothers hurried their children indoors. Hand in hand, Inga and the boy reached the village, breathless. Amid the commotion, Laughing Friend gestured in the direction they had last seen the raven taunting the cubs. He spoke in a stream of rapid, excited words. Shining Eyes joined the circle and listened, spellbound.

Laughing Friend told the story of the raven. He flapped his arms for raven wings and imitated the bird's outbursts. Inga saw the drama played by the raven now re-created by her friend. The onlookers raised their eyebrows, fascinated. Whale Tooth and Broken Smile spoke quickly to the men. Soon a band of hunters, armed with weapons, sped toward the place of the bear encounter. Those people left behind fell silent as they watched the hunters disappear.

Inga searched the sky. There was no sign of the raven yet. In time, they heard the distant shouts of the hunters. The sky remained empty. After what seemed an endless wait to Inga, the men returned. They murmured calm words to their families. Evidently, the bears had fled. The hunters pointed off in the direction they had come from and told their story.

The children who sneaked outside again still trembled and clung to their mothers' knees. Everyone buzzed with chatter. Did they wonder about the raven, too? Inga stood to one side, silent, mournful. She felt a terrible emptiness inside. Laughing Friend's eyes were also fixed on the sky. Yes, she thought, he cared about the raven. The raven must not die.

At long last, she caught sight of a flight of ravens flapping overhead. Was her raven among them? She watched keenly as the birds headed over the village. "Look!" she cried. Laughing Friend yelped and called to the villagers. One raven left the others. Inga thought she recognized the long, feathery wingtips. People called out in joyous voices. But was it Inga's raven? The bird coasted down from above – yes! – and landed on her shoulder as if nothing whatsoever had happened. He blinked at the onlookers and started to preen his feathers. "Grawwk!" he declared.

The Bear People circled the raven. They chattered at the bird. The raven rocked his head from side to side and let out a playful "Grawwwww! Grawwwww!" People laughed. Inga took a deep, happy breath of relief. Her heart floated back into its accustomed place, since the raven was at her side again, safe and well. He was a hero.

The raven should have a reward, Inga thought. He loved berries. Now was the perfect time to show off her new word in the Bear People's language. Carefully she pronounced it. The villagers stepped closer, as if they had not heard her clearly. Inga proudly repeated her word.

Whale Tooth looked at Shining Eyes. Blue Shell looked at her daughter Silk Hair. Inga brought out her leather purse and emptied the last berries into her hand. These the raven gobbled up. She tried to make a face that said, "See? Berries." Inga prompted her hearers with the new word once more. Suddenly Silk Hair darted away. Moments later Red Shoes and then Cricket raced off, as well. She hadn't really meant for them to bring her more berries, she thought, but all of this showed that learning the Bear People's language was not going to be that hard, after all.

Silk Hair hurried back to the scene. Oddly enough, she held up a pair of skin boots. Red Shoes and Cricket raced each other to the circle of friends once more. Each also carried a pair of boots. With a chuckle, Laughing Friend tugged off one of his own boots, held it up and chirped the word she had thought meant berries. The villagers now chanted happily, "Boots, boots."

Inga remembered back to the way she had pointed at the berries at her feet, and at the same time, of course, to her boots. Her face reddened deeply. She tried to look pleased with the villagers' approval. "Boots," she murmured. Yet, for some reason, she found it impossible not to laugh. She had succeeded in learning a new word, she told herself. There would be other new words, and the Bear People appeared to be happy to share their language with her.

The raven hopped to Laughing Friend's wrist and pecked at the boy's fingers. "Aii!" the boy yipped. Laughing Friend gave the bird a bit of fish. The onlookers laughed as the bird chortled. Whale Tooth held out a morsel of meat, and the raven again croaked his thanks. Soon others offered the hero his reward of berries and beetles. Inga knew the raven had helped these people accept a strange girl into their midst. They also were happy the bird had returned safely from the bear encounter.

Laughing Friend was especially glad the raven had returned. For an instant, she thought she spotted a single tear fall from his eye. He quickly left the group and returned to his house, alone. She found the boy sitting just inside the doorway. As usual, he was working at carving something. He deepened a small hollow in the round stone that had briefly been his weapon. As he carved, he did not look up to greet her.

Was he jealous of the raven's triumph? she wondered. No, she understood. The boy had come to love the raven, just as she did. Some might not think this fitting in a boy who wanted so much to be grown up. So he sat here carving a hole in the stone. She recognized that he was making a stone lamp. This hole would be filled with whale blubber. Quietly, she sat beside him as he worked. The raven had made them friends.

Chapter Seven

The Silver Penny

Southern Labrador

Weeks later, Broken Smile hurried up the path from the shore, shouting something excitedly to his neighbours. He grinned broadly, revealing the gap left by his missing tooth. At his words, commotion erupted.

The raven mumbled curious questions in Inga's ear. "I don't know," she told him. "We'll see what's happening."

Laughing Friend gestured toward the shore. Inga saw that a boat of the same design as the Bear People's own approached. The villagers crowded together at the head of the path as two young men landed their craft. Obviously well known to the Bear People, the young men dressed in the same manner. Inga thought back to the boat she and Laughing Friend had seen weeks ago from the berrying place. Evidently, she thought, there were other villages of the Bear People, and not far away.

Whatever the young men called out as they approached, everyone who heard them burst into furious conversation. The first messenger to reach them was a thin young man with long hair. He swept his arm toward the afternoon sun and unleashed a loud stream of syllables. Everyone was aflame with excitement. The second messenger was a short, square-shouldered fellow, and he, too, spoke in emphatic words that stirred his hearers to action.

"I don't understand," Inga whispered to the raven who pecked at her ear. She listened carefully to the flying words of the villagers, but they spoke with such agitation that she recognized only a few of the new words she had learned. The village became a frenzy of activity. Men grasped spears and knives and rushed to their boats.

A thought suddenly gripped Inga's throat. Dare she hope? Could this be the moment she had longed for? They have seen a ship, Inga told herself. Surely, only a Norse ship and Norsemen sailing it could create this excitement.

She must not be left behind. Whale Tooth flung orders in every direction. Inga darted out of his sight, so he would not send her away. She ran to Laughing Friend and tugged at his elbow. To her joy, Laughing Friend took her hand

and pulled her toward the boats. Yes! She was in luck. He would take her with him! Did he understand she wanted to go home? Thrilled, Inga ran down the path. The raven burst from her shoulder and sailed into the sky.

Inga and the boy tumbled into Whale Tooth's boat that soon hastened down the coastline, the rowers charging the waves vigorously. The Bear People's boats moved like cheerful porpoises, and their occupants shouted, calling to friends in the other boats. Overhead the raven followed the expedition. Inga saw no other young people among them, not even the two boys Grasshopper and Cricket. Yet, fortunately, Laughing Friend was in the party, probably as an honour due Whale Tooth's son, she thought, and she was his friend. Spray fanned over the boats, showering the passengers. Everyone bubbled with agitation.

Could the ship have come from Greenland, maybe even from her own settlement, to search for survivors of the shipwreck? Or had Uncle Knut lingered here to look for Inga and the others? Inga's heart throbbed with every slap of the waves against the prow. If only their captain, Arne Stefansson, and the others had made camp somewhere! As the boat pushed on, the stone spindle whorl in her necklace beat against her pounding heart. She felt the rhythm mock her own breath. This was the moment she had waited for!

Inga resolved that as soon as she saw the first glimpse of a Norse ship or person on the shore, she was determined to stand and shout a warning. The Bear People had been kind to her, but now they gripped their weapons and their faces were contorted with the passion of their quest. Surely they planned an attack. Was she to be their hostage?

The spray cooled her feverish cheeks as the boat forged on. Passing rocks and cliffs, they deftly dodged rocks and shoals. Whale Tooth paddled from the stern, guiding their path, his glance fixed ahead. He roared orders to the others, who followed his directions at once. Paddling at the prow, Red Shoes never paused with each flashing stroke. The sun bowed toward the west, silver and brilliant. Everyone squinted at the blinding sea-path. The sea quivered with light. In all the boats, the paddlers soon fell silent, concentrating. Inga heard only the wind, the rush of water against the hull, and from time to time the crying of the raven overhead.

Following Whale Tooth's lead, they all edged around the point. For the first time she could see people along the shore hailing them, waving, hobbling over rocks. They were evidently Bear People from another village. A few of their dogs splashed beside them at the water's edge.

Laughing Friend craned to listen to the two messengers who had summoned the villagers and whose boat came alongside their own. The messengers called out and gestured ahead. We must be close now, Inga thought.

Drawing strength from the commotion, Red Shoes ploughed the waves so that their boat shot well ahead of the others. More figures scurried along the shore. Inga squinted in the sun, searching for a familiar sight. Then she saw a silhouette offshore, a long, dark, curving shape. Shielding her eyes from the sun, she leaned forward so far that Laughing Friend reached out to keep her from falling.

Yes, even in the glare, she saw it: a long, dark shape.

But it was not the shape of a Norse ship, its sail bursting with wind, though the image lying in the waves was familiar. As her heart sank, those of her companions rose in merriment. People ashore called out their greetings. They chanted a word over and over. Its meaning was obvious to her. "*Hval,*" she whispered in her own language. Whale. A great whale had beached and died stranded on the shore.

Numb with disappointment, Inga climbed out on the land. At once everyone set to work. Laughing Friend ran off to follow his father's instructions. Waves lapped against the sleek, tremendous body of the whale, as long as a Norse longhouse back home. She felt a pang of sympathy for the poor creature, stranded, unable to return home and finally defeated.

Inga did not even smile when the raven alighted on the top of the carcass, strutted and whistled. With his thick beak, the bird pecked a hole in the smooth skin, tore off a piece of fat and let out a happy croak before gobbling it up. Onlookers laughed, enchanted.

The Bear People gathered the precious whale blubber

that would provide light and heat through the winter months. They cut strips of fat and meat. The bone and teeth would be harvested to make many objects, from spearheads and knives to spoons and combs. Nothing would go to waste.

More boats arrived. Women came with pots and bowls and baskets. Even small children came. They played in the water, running and tossing pebbles. The whale was a wonderful gift from the sea. It would have been to Inga's people, too, she reminded herself.

Her spirit glum, Inga sat high on the bank in the dry grass, legs tucked close, arms hugging her knees. She saw nothing of the turmoil below but gazed out on the horizon at the sun-spattered sea. Her gaze fell from this sight for only an instant, when the raven appeared and lighted on her shoulder. If she was sad, he decided to be sad, too.

That night many stories were told around the fire. Usually Inga liked to watch the animated faces of the storytellers and the drama of their gestures, imagining what the tales might describe. Shadows from the fire fluttered over faces and hands. Yet this night she paid little attention.

The villagers and their visitors enjoyed the rich whale meat. Children gnawed bones, and the precious marrow inside the bones was treasured by many as the best of treats. Dogs savoured the tidbits tossed to them, though they took care to keep out of the raven's range. Even the raven sat on a rock and picked at a bit of meat he held with his feet.

The people from the other village joined them for the night, obviously close friends with Whale Tooth's people. One was a slim, shy woman who resembled Shining Eyes and Blue Shell so much that Inga wondered if she could be a cousin or even a sister to one of them. The three women sat together whispering and laughing.

Inga could not listen to any of this. For hours she had been making her plan. She must act. She crept up the bank above the fire ring where Laughing Friend busied himself drawing on the flat stones with the charred pieces he kept in a skin bag. Peeking over his shoulder she saw that he drew pictures of the day's adventure. The raven floated down to the boy's feet and watched, too.

On one rock the boy had drawn the village with its rounded dwellings. His mother stood waving to the arriving visitors in their boats. On the next rock stood a sketch of the headland and his father's boat in the lead, rounding the point. Upon a third rock he drew the beached whale on the shore. To Inga the whale looked remarkably large, but that was probably because it was so important to the Bear People. The boy looked up and smiled.

She told him, "You are an artist." He seemed to understand that she praised him, for he looked away shyly. He went on to draw people working at the shore, their boats upturned now. With a grin at Inga, he added a small figure with a dark bird perched on its shoulder.

Inga smiled and nodded. "Yes, I know. You are drawing me. *Meg*. Inga." His eyebrows curled when she pronounced her name, she noticed. The word "Inga" was not easy for him. She pointed to herself in the drawing. "You drew a picture of me. Inga," she said. "That means me. *Meg*." She pointed to herself.

The boy sat up, interested. "*Mah-ee*," he repeated, drawing out the vowel in a startlingly unnatural way to her ears. When she pronounced the word *meg*, there was only a whisper of an "ee" sound at the end. He pointed to her. "*Mah-ee!*" he repeated happily.

Suddenly she understood his excitement. He took this to be her name. She nodded. "Yes," she agreed, "*meg*." Then she pronounced it, as he did. "*Mah-ee*." She asked, "May I draw?" She took a charred marker and placed another figure next to her own in the picture. This figure wore a necklace of shells and feathers. The boy cried out, pleased, and gestured at himself. "Yes," Inga said, gesturing toward him. "You. I call you Laughing Friend." She smiled but knew he did not understand. "I call you that because you laughed at the raven and became his friend. You are my friend now, too."

He pointed at the picture of himself and uttered a difficult cluster of syllables. But she could not yet attempt his name.

Now he touched both pictures. He indicated himself, speaking his name, and beside him: "*Mah-ee*."

"*Mah-ee*," she answered. "That will be a good name

for me." She wondered if she would ever be able to teach him her real name or learn his, explaining why she had first called him Laughing Friend.

Now it is time for another picture, she told herself. She cleared the sand from a nearby stone. By the leaping firelight she drew the Bear People's village, although she knew it was not with the same skill as the boy's. She drew two figures standing at the shore, watching the horizon.

Before she could identify them, the boy pointed from the pictures to each of them. "*Mah-ee*," he said when he gestured toward her.

As she drew, he watched intently. Now she added a ship on the horizon.

"Hoh," the boy whispered.

The raven tried to nip the smudgy embers from her hand, but she pushed him gently aside. "*Nei*," she told him. "No."

Cautiously she put a mast and then a square sail on the ship. The boy squinted. What is this? he seemed to wonder. She hoped that sometime he had seen such sails, or at least heard about them. The ship sailed close to the shore as she drew it surrounded by lilting waves, sturdy and impressive with graceful lines of curved, overlapping timbers. She drew the stout, useful ship of Norse traders, not a high-prowed warriors' ship. The large square sail of *wadmal*, carefully treated cloth, swelled with the wind. Aboard the ship she added silhouettes of people.

The boy's mouth was pressed in a tight line as he

watched her drawing unfold. An anchor line showed that the ship had come to rest, and she drew a point of land nearby. She added the outline of houses on the land. But what sort of camp would the Greenlanders have built? She decided to make the structures resemble the farmhouses back home: turf-walled houses with peaked roofs, doorways edged with stout timber, and square smoke holes neatly set in the rooftops. She drew smoke drifting into the air.

Again the raven tried to filch a bit of charred ember, but she lifted him to her shoulder. "This is not a game," she scolded. The boy's face remained expectant but solemn. She added the figures of her people standing on the shore, dressed in their Norse clothing.

"Hah!" he cried. He grabbed a charred bit and rapidly added more figures, men with beards.

"Yes!" Inga declared. "These are my people! This is where I must go. I need your help!" If only he could understand! Now she added a small boat to one side of the picture. Its occupants, two small figures, watched the activity of the Norse arrival. "*Mah-ee,*" she told him, indicating herself watching from the small boat. From his figure in the picture she pointed to Laughing Friend. "You." Then she showed herself, now walking on the shore, the raven on her shoulder, approaching the Norsemen.

The boy frowned. "Aagh!" he exclaimed, frowning. With a swift hand he erased the heads of the Norsemen and set to work in an amazing task: he gave them new heads! Inga leaned closer. She gasped. The boy drew her people, but now they had the heads of wolves! Wolves! She knew what he was telling her, that to him they were Wolf People!

He tapped the images of the Wolf People and uttered harsh words. What did he mean? Was he thinking of some old story Broken Smile liked to tell? Was it a story of trolls and spirits? Why were they Wolf People?

Inga tried to make the venture less bold. She drew a large boulder with both of them and the raven hiding behind it, watching the Norsemen. Would he dare go as close as that?

Laughing Friend plucked up a marker and this time he made the connection unmistakable. He added more characters who stepped ashore from the boats. On every one he drew the head of a wolf. Instead of hands and feet he gave them wolves' claws. Energetically, he rubbed out the image of the boy and girl and the raven observing from behind the boulder. Instead he drew his own face with a look of great fear. He uttered a painful moan. The raven mimicked the boy's cry with a fearful croak. Wolf People! the boy tried to tell her.

Inga sat back, taking this in. Below them, around the fire, the Bear People laughed and chattered. Whale Tooth was the storyteller now, and his listeners were rapt with attention. In their eyes fire sparkled. Children in their parents' laps had fallen asleep, for the exciting day had been too long. She had thought of these people as beasts with human legs, their heads those of the great snow bears, the most ferocious of bears.

"*Nei*," she replied to Laughing Friend, gazing at his drawing, "these are not Wolf People." But how could she tell him that her people were good and kind? How could she make a visit to the Norse camp, wherever it was, less threatening?

Inga lay the charred stick down. She tried another idea. She emptied her leather purse and motioned to him to take whatever he wanted. He fingered the piece of woven cloth, the small whetstone for sharpening needles and scissors, and other trinkets. He lifted the silver penny, squeezed it, tapped it, and held it up to the light.

"Take it," Inga urged. "It's yours." She traced her finger over the picture of herself and Laughing Friend going to the Norse camp. "We will go in the boat," she said, following the route in the drawing. "Take what you want," she said. "We two will go."

He frowned. "Aagh!" he exclaimed, tapping the heads of the Wolf People. He shoved the silver penny back in her hand. There was no prize that would make him venture into the camp of the Wolf People.

"I know," she said softly. "It was wrong to ask you." Gently she rubbed away the image of the journey. She replaced this with a vision of the Bear People's village and herself and the boy side by side.

Inga lifted the spindle whorl, the stone that hung from the necklace he had given her. She said, gesturing between them, "You gave me this as a gift." Then she placed the penny in his hand. "*Mah-ee* gives you this. You are my friend, and that is enough."

Laughing Friend's words seemed to thank her. He took the penny and examined its ornamented face in the light once more.

The raven jumped to the boy's knee and nibbled the bright coin. The boy laughed but held the silver penny firmly. The boy and the raven played together, teasing one another. Inga turned away. Weary and downcast, she glanced toward the fireside and watched the shadows and the light flicker.

"I must go alone," she whispered.

Chapter Eight

The Bone Needle

A hunting camp, Newfoundland

One winter morning the raven woke Inga with happy gurgles even before the first inkling of dawn. He loved the snow, and a thick mantle had fallen in the night. The raven played in snow as some birds play in puddles. He rolled on it and flapped his wings. Over her cap, Inga pulled the fur-lined hood of the garment that Watching Eyes had sewn for her. Winter could be beautiful, she thought, despite the icy cold. The wind felt fresh against her face.

The site of their hunting camp was an open place with a broad view, for the thickets of twisted trees lay far back from the shore. Hunting parties ventured out from the settlements only on short expeditions now, for storms moved in unexpectedly. Soon it would be too dangerous to go out at all. Back in the village, people spent much time in the snug turf and stone houses. On the bitterest days no one budged from them. The narrow entrance passage in Whale Tooth's house helped keep out the cold.

Here in the camp, the hunters gathered, talking over their plans. The days were so short now the hunters had to set out as soon as they could.

Inga set out to look for animal tracks and to watch the horizon where the sky was indistinct in the grey hour. On a nearby twig, the raven settled. He fluffed his wings to capture air that would help keep him warm. The raven greeted her with playful words. They strolled the rising bank.

Inga caught sight of Laughing Friend walking the edge of the shore. He had apparently forgotten about their discussion months ago of the Wolf People, as he seemed to think of them. She was glad. She knew the boy feared the Norse as she had feared the Bear People. They had learned these lessons from infancy. He did not realize that she was one of them, and his friendship was precious. If it were her fate to spend her life among the Bear People, she would need the strength of his friendship. She shivered. Stay here? Forever? She could never believe that would happen. Never. One day her ship must appear on the horizon. She wondered how far away lay *ginnungagap*, the great abyss at the end of the world. She hoped it was a long way and that no ship would ever come near it.

Inga turned toward a summoning voice.

"*Mah-ee!*" Laughing Friend stumbled through the snow toward her.

Now she could reply to him in his language, greeting him and inviting him up to the top of the bank. She recognized the word for "boat" as he gestured like a fish slipping through the water. "Ah, we're going in the boats today," she said. She knew what her duty would be. While the hunters trekked into the brush or along the ice in the inlets, she would watch the boats. If the hunters were lucky, they might catch a seal in the last of the migration south.

They found Shining Eyes stocking the boats with supplies, even though the party intended to return the same day. If they were caught in a storm they would need food to survive. She knew now that Shining Eyes was Blue Shell's youngest sister. Inga had learned much from both of these women.

Soon the raven was flying ahead of the boats, as if he sensed the hunters' direction before they did. Red Shoes paddled from the prow in front of Inga, and Cut Eye paddled in the stern. The wind was already brisk, and the rowers laboured to keep their direction. Even in the early winter, floating ice could be dangerous. They had to keep careful watch. With a grin on his face, Red Shoes tried to outdo the other boats. Whale Tooth spoke a few insistent words to the irrepressible young man. Red Shoes, like

Grasshopper and Cricket, had been increasingly compelled to leave his boyish games to help with the important tasks of the village. Laughing Friend carried his bows and arrows to help with the hunt. The boys were growing up. Inga thought that was why Whale Tooth was not in a playful mood.

The boats were helpful in crossing to an island or over a channel, but much of the expedition involved walking over their hunting territory. The boats might lie alone for hours, so her task was not unimportant, she tried to convince herself. The morning grew clearer, and, though windy, there was no sign of a storm. This would be a good hunting day, she decided.

The raven dropped down and perched on the prow where Red Shoes boldly plied his paddle. At last, they came to a bushy highland above a cove. By a shallow shore, among scattered rocks, the banks were wet from trickling springs. Footprints revealed where animals had come down to the shore to search for food or to drink from the springs that emptied into the sea. One boulder shaded a portion of the bank so that it shone with ice and snow. The raven leapt from the boat and landed on the high boulder. He tumbled down the snow slide, whooping and cackling. From the bottom, he fluttered to the top once more then skidded down again, wings flapping, and chortling gaily. Even Whale Tooth laughed at his jolly performance.

The men paused to watch until the raven stopped and whisked himself aloft with a croak. He saw something. Cut

Eye spotted rabbits dashing for cover. The boats pulled for shore. Except for Laughing Friend, the hunters dashed into the brush and disappeared. The boy stopped to help Inga take charge of the boats. They hauled them on land and hid them in the brush.

The two friends then climbed to the top of the boulder for a look but saw no one, though they could hear shouts of their distant companions. As for the raven, he returned to his snow slide. Inga took in the view of the broad meadow. Her Norse ship had never reached Vinland. But wherever it was, it might have looked like this, she thought. Grass poked through the snow for some distance. Here was good pasture for livestock, and that would be important for the Norsemen. She saw two ponds and a stream that burbled vigorously across the land. There were useful bays and inlets, too. Here people could raise sheep, goats and cattle, but the Bear People had none of these animals, and she realized how fortunate the people of her homeland had been.

"*Ravn!*" she cried, searching the scene. The bird sprang from the brush and into the sky above their heads, sailing above the two friends as they crossed the snowy land. But soon a cluster of grouse exploded from the grassy hummocks. The boy notched his arrow and crept away in pursuit. He would leave the boats to her now.

When he was out of sight, Inga rambled on, in the opposite direction from the hunters. Ahead of her, the raven scouted the land, crossing back and forth. Inga noticed something fluttering in the distance. "*Ravn*, what is it?" she called. The bird swooped and soon returned. He held a feather in his beak, the fringed down of a gosling.

The goose nesting site they found was long deserted, as Inga knew it would be. The geese were far away in their winter home. The frisky wind rustled bits of down caught in the brush. More down threaded the large rings of the nests. She knew that it was not from the goslings but from their mothers who plucked the down from their own plumage to make the nests soft and warm.

"We have found a treat," Inga told the raven, starting to gather the fluffy bits. The bird lighted on an empty nest and poked at the deep bowl of its centre. "We will make many things with this down, but first we must collect it." She slipped off her hood to remove her cap and pack it with down. The raven joined in the game and pulled loose down from the nests, though sometimes Inga had to chase after the fluffy down in the wind. When the cap was tightly filled, Inga bound it with the strings and tied it around her neck. Then she began filling the leather purse.

The raven plucked a thick ball of down, but when he mumbled to get her attention, the down worked loose and the stiff wind whisked it aloft and away. "Catch it," Inga cried, laughing. Following the floating down, her gaze caught sight of another distant bright object, this time sailing in the dark blue of the sea.

"Ohh, it's a boat!" She studied it carefully. Could she believe what she thought she saw? She scrambled over the clearing. Yes, it was one of their boats! Somehow it had worked itself loose. How terrible if she lost it! She tumbled through the snow toward the bank. She shouted in the direction Laughing Friend had taken. "Come! Our boat!" She called to the raven, "Go! Find him!" The raven fled with rapid wings.

Inga slipped down the bank toward the water. She thrust out a hand and found a protruding root, catching herself before reaching the shoreline. As she picked herself up, she saw a slick muddy path left by the boat that had slid down as the springs loosened it and sent the boat skidding to the shore. "That's how it happened," she muttered. What would Whale Tooth say if she lost a boat? This had been her only responsibility and she had failed.

Among the distant dots of rock, the straying boat idly wandered, bumping one rock then another. She knew she must reach it before the boat pushed free into deep water. In this wind she knew she could not paddle out in another boat to catch it, not alone anyway. Alone she was not strong enough to control the boat. If only Laughing Friend would come. Was he lost? Why didn't the raven return? The boat spun around and settled against a rock. It quivered in the wind. Yes, she might just reach it, if she acted at once. Jumping from rock to rock, she could make it. She must make it.

Inga stumbled along the rocky shore until she found a long stick that had drifted ashore and was now tough and dry. Using the stick to steady herself, she stepped on the nearest stone, then on to another and another. She followed the rocks like a pathway through a forest. Before putting her full weight on a stone, she tried each one gingerly, eyeing the surface for slippery spots. At last she reached the rock closest to the boat. Her heart sank. "From the shore it looked so close," she whispered. In fact, a sizable gap separated her from the prow and from the rock the boat rested against, for the moment. Though she tried to reach the boat with the long stick, the gap was too wide. The water was too deep to wade and far too cold to swim. She glanced at the shore. There was no sight of Laughing Friend. She must think what to do.

Another pattern of stones showed itself to her. This path led around the boat and finally to a stone near the other end of the boat. Was it near enough?

Inga wasted no time in re-tracing her route until it joined another widely arching curve of rocks leading toward the stern. "Uhh!" she exclaimed as her foot found a wobbly stone. But the stick steadied her, just in time. She tried another smaller stone. That one proved solid.

As Inga reached the rock nearest the stern of the boat, the fitful wind shifted. Inga watched, frantic. The boat shivered. "Come here, little boat!" she begged. "Don't leave me." The rock she stood on was narrow. She held the stick in both hands, getting her balance. Then the boat began to turn in her direction, edging ever so slowly. From somewhere the raven dropped out of the sky and landed on the stern. He croaked and flapped his wings.

Inga held out her stick to its full length and touched the boat, coaxing it toward her. The raven hopped to the boat's rim and grabbed the stick in his beak. "Hold on!" Inga urged. Slowly she pulled the boat until it just reached her grasp. She felt the wind try to turn it, but she and the raven held fast. When it veered close enough, Inga crawled over the edge and tumbled inside. She had saved the boat!

She righted herself and looked back to the shore. There was Laughing Friend slipping down the bank. He shouted something. He ran along the water's edge, waving. For the first time, Inga realized with horror that there was no paddle in the boat and, when she had climbed in, the boat had been jarred loose from the rock and floated freely away. But she did have her stick. With an excited gasp, she saw two stones ahead she could grab. She must rescue herself and the boat, she thought. She must snag one of them, for beyond her lay the immense open sea. Menacing white foam scarred the dark surface.

Poising her stick at the side of the boat, she gave herself a moment to glance at the shore. The boy mimicked just what she intended to do: pole herself to land from rock to rock. He started toward her, hopping from stone to stone. As the first rock neared, Inga positioned herself in the prow, her stick ready. Just as she leaned out, about to spear the rock and steady the gliding boat, a gust batted the prow. The boat headed toward deep water.

"Agghh!" she heard the boy cry. His shriek echoed over the snowy land.

Inga leaned over as far as she could. The stone was out of reach. Helplessly she saw the boat sail on and the boy's image, as he stood waving on a rock, grow smaller and smaller. But there, some distance ahead, protruding out of the water, one last jagged rock stood in their watery path. There was hope! The boat briskly skimmed the water. The raven flew ahead. He made for the jutting stone, lighted on it and stood, flapping and croaking. Inga leaned over, feeling the lightweight craft lean with her. The rock shot past, well beyond reach, but she realized at once she could never have braced the moving boat with her stick at that speed, if, indeed, the rock had not bashed a hole in the skin covering.

The raven glided from the rock and dropped down on the prow of the drifting boat. His gleaming eyes scanned the disappearing land behind them. Inga could see Laughing Friend suddenly turn back and run, run as fast as he could, away from her. Of course, he was going for help. He was smart in his decision, she knew. He had not yielded to the impulse to row after her alone in the rough wind, for if he should be unsuccessful or stranded, too, then it would be hours before their companions would know that they were missing. In seconds he was out of sight, masked by the high headland. There was nothing she could do now but sit and watch.

The boat rushed on, caught in the power of the current. She kept alert for dangerous ice drifts and held her stick at the ready. Inlets passed by. A gnarled forest and knolls arose far up on the land. Twice, the light craft spun completely around in the current. From time to time, in its path, the boat veered closer to shore for a moment, and Inga tried to reach the bottom with her stick. The water always remained too deep. Of course, there could be no question of swimming ashore, even holding to the side of the boat, for the water was treacherously cold and the currents deadly. Even if she made it to land, she would freeze there in no time. She saw no one. Only the retreating land. Only the sea.

Soon she might wander out to open water, forever lost. She sat and watched the distant blue spectre of the land. The raven sat with her. She grew cold, hungry. The appearance of the land continually changed and finally flattened, though high cliffs arose from long fingers of headland reaching out into the sea. The day was fading when a sharp promontory appeared ahead. The currents changed, and the boat veered toward the misty shore. Inga gripped the sides tightly as the boat rocked in the agitated water. Waves nudged her toward land. Ahead breakers unravelled their foamy grins. If she were swept toward shore, would the boat be crushed by unseen rocks and shoals?

"Kraaaaa!" the raven cried.

Yes, those were shallows ahead, though she saw no protruding rock through the mist. Her throat tightening, Inga hoped she might reach the bottom with her stick. And then what? Ahead, in the shadow of the cove a shape appeared. Is that what the raven saw? Was it a bear not yet asleep in its winter den? Then another silhouette loomed through the fog above the curve of the land, then another. The raven muttered dark words. He saw these mysterious forms, too. But these were not bears. They remained unmoving, growing larger as Inga and the raven blew toward the coast. Had the boat taken them to another of the Bear People's villages? If so, she might yet be saved.

The boat circled the headland. Mist hovering over the snow hid the land in the arc of the cove. But the watery path ahead demanded her attention. What seemed to be a sandbar lay there, and waves spilled over the shallows with a soft, "Chuuu, chuuu, chuuu." Concentrating all her remaining strength and courage, Inga poised her stick over the side. It was then that she could not deny a stolen glance at the land. Dark forms arose now out of the mist. They pointed to the sky, tapered like fir trees. They were roofs! Not the rounded roofs of the Bear People's houses – but Norse roofs! Stunned, Inga fell back in the boat, its prow soon thumping against the sandbar so that the boat lurched to a stop.

She saw these structures on the coastline as if they had been ghosts. She struggled to find her breath. Had she strayed so far as the world of the spirits? There! There were Norse boat sheds. Above them, on higher ground, arose more buildings, their steeply pitched roofs thick and pierced by smoke holes. The houses were like those of her village in Greenland. Norse houses! This was unmistakably a Norse settlement.

Her heart pounded. She knelt in the boat, paralyzed with astonishment. Shouts jumped from her throat. "Help! Help!" she shrieked. "I'm out here! Help me!" The raven caught her panic and leapt into the air, croaking madly.

A large wave tossed the boat loose from the sand, and the incoming sea spun her toward land. Shaken into alertness, Inga drove her stick into the water – and touched bottom! Quickly she steadied the craft, planted her stick again and again and pushed the boat toward shore. The boat lifted and fell with each wave until it reached the breaking waves. She gave a mighty push with the stick, propelling the boat until it glided against the pebbled bottom. She leapt from the boat and raced up the slope.

"Here!" she hollered. "Help, I'm down here!" Up above the village, the raven circled the rooftops. His frantic alarms echoed. Her own heart leapt. Excitement raced through her body.

Her eyes caressed the scene joyously. These were sights she had despaired of ever seeing again. There were the smoke holes neatly framed with wood. The doors, under straight stout beams for lintels, were formed of smooth wooden planks. The houses stood in a crescent formation. Nearby, the boat sheds were just as they might have appeared back home, though not so numerous. That small building on the crest of the slope looked like the forge. Perhaps another was a bath house.

"*Hallo! Hallo!*" she cried, running over the grass. "Help, I've been lost! I sailed with Arne Stefansson and our ship was wrecked in a storm!" She headed for the longhouse at the end of the crescent of buildings. In this great house she knew she would find many people, maybe some from her own village. The raven swooped over the peaked roofs, crying out. Inga threw herself against the sturdy door and tumbled inside and to the floor. Something sharp pierced her hand as she fell. But she clambered to her knees immediately. "It is I...I, Inga Sigurdsdottir! I've been searching for—"

Then she gasped in shock, for her eyes gazed on a long chamber and on the doorways of adjoining rooms, on the large stone cooking area, on benches and on stout pillars. All strung with cobwebs. Overhead, the roof, torn with holes, glinted with the light of the sky. Mice skittered into the shadows, snowflakes tumbled in from the draft of the doorway. The long silent room stood utterly deserted. There was no whiff of a fire, no sound of sheep or goats in a pen nearby, no chatter of women at their sewing.

Shaken, Inga staggered to the doorway. Why had she not noticed? The yard was blanketed in snow that no footstep, except her own, had touched. Beneath the snow, tufts of grass crouched where once there must have been a worn path to each threshold. Not even one boat lay at the shore or in the sheds. No rope or sail dried in the wind. Above the doorway, birds had built nests, and these, too, were long abandoned.

Heartbroken, Inga roamed the encampment. In the forge lay cold black lumps of iron slag. The raven hopped up to the flat stone that served as an anvil. Here, rivets and nails to repair the ships had been made. She saw a kiln for making charcoal, now empty, cold.

Mute with despair, Inga returned to the longhouse and walked its length and breadth, the raven strutting after her. She touched the cold embers in the hearth. The raven nudged small, discoloured bones, protruding from the ashes. They were old and dusty. He flung them aside. She and Grandmother had visited old abandoned farms in Greenland where life had been too lonely for people to hold on. They had looked like this. This was a village of ghosts. And even the ghosts had left.

As Inga dragged her steps to the threshold, something caught her eye in the light. The raven trotted to her side as she knelt to examine the object. This was what had pricked her hand earlier. "A needle," she whispered. This was a Norse bone needle with a drilled eye. A woman must have been in a hurry to have been so careless as to lose this valuable possession. Inga opened her leather purse and brought out the scrap of red cloth that had once held a broken needle. Now she speared the cloth with the good bone needle. She closed the door behind her. With her fingers, she rubbed the leather purse and felt the bone needle inside. If somehow she could make her way back to the Bear People, she would keep this needle, the last object she would have to remind her of her own Norse people. She swallowed this thought and its taste was bitter.

In the boat shed she found a rope and a tall, sturdy pole. With the pole, Inga pushed the boat slowly and carefully along the edge of the shore, just far enough out to keep from grazing the hull. The rope she fastened to the boat so that she might lead it along the rocky spots where she could not risk adding her own weight. The raven perched on the prow, keeping watch. She hoped the Bear People would not think her already gone to their land of the dead. The sun sagged lower in the sky, wrapping her and the bird in icy cold.

After a long time, she rounded a point and was poling the boat along a muddy stretch when a cry stirred the air. A dark silhouette appeared down the coast. A shout rippled over the water. Inga stood, her pole firmly stuck in the water. *"Mah-ee!"* the voice called. Unexpectedly, she found tears warming her cheeks.

Whale Tooth hailed her with a vigorous wave and a greeting. *"Mah-ee!"* his voice echoed. Plying his paddle at the prow was Laughing Friend. In moments their able strokes brought them alongside. Laughing Friend lashed the two boats together, and Whale Tooth lifted her into his boat. A stream of words cascaded from his mouth as he embraced her as warmly as any father ever held a lost child. He dried her tears. Whale Tooth murmured gentle words to calm her, wrapped her in a bearskin, and settled her at his knee. Shyly, Laughing Friend returned to his post, glancing at her with softly gleaming eyes and a tender smile. Whale Tooth gestured decisively toward their new direction. At once, father and son sped to the site where their companions waited.

The next day, the hunters headed back to the Bear People's camp together. Laughing Friend had caught a fat bundle of grouse. The others rejoiced that they had found seals, many rabbits, various game birds and a fox. Most of all, they celebrated her return. The day was grey and chill, the weak sun scarcely visible behind clouds. Inga and Laughing Friend huddled under the bearskin. Cold, sharp flakes brushed Inga's face, but she felt safe here among the Bear People.

Chapter Nine

The Whetstone

Southern Labrador

our more winters passed by before, once again, springtime warmth restored the land of the Bear People. All its beauty shone clear. The raven floated lazily overhead, basking in the comforting sun, talking loudly with other ravens and sporting with them through the sky. He patrolled the air every day, waiting for migrating birds. It was his role to greet them, croaking as each flight came in sight. He soared high and if migrants came to rest at the shore, he cackled away at them, from a distance. Between these duties he accompanied Inga, whether she was packing the hunters' boats with provisions or searching the shore for firewood.

One afternoon, the little children helped Inga gather wood. While they walked the beach, they made a game of naming the last passing ice floes for the animals they resembled. Some of these fantastic contortions of ice were blue, others green or pink. All of them were mysterious and beautiful.

"No climbing on the ice," Inga warned the little ones who clawed at the enormous jumbles of ice stranded at the water's edge. These days the jumbles were unstable. "That's too dangerous," she explained.

"We'll be good, *Mah-ee*," they promised. Obediently the children flitted on to another game, for they were tired anyway of comparing the ice to frogs and fish.

Weeks ago the children first heard the ice growl and crack as it began breaking up. They had cried out, "Wolves! Wolves! *Mah-ee*, tell the black bird to save us!" The raven was a favourite part of any game.

"If wolves come," Inga had assured them, "the bird will nip their tails."

Bearskin Girl had agreed. "Feathered brother can talk wolf language," she told the little ones. "He'll tell them to go away."

Bearskin Girl, as Inga still thought of her, was growing up into a smart girl. She was old enough now to help with the littlest children, as she did today, piling their bits of wood along the shore. To Inga, the girl's clear-eyed face was beautiful. When the villagers learned that Silk Hair and Red Shoes were to have their first baby in the summer, Bearskin Girl changed, Inga had noticed. Silk Hair was her cousin, and when Bearskin Girl looked at Silk Hair now she seemed impatient to grow up, too. She played little. Instead she asked Inga to teach her to sew. Whale Tooth said proudly that there were two big girls in the family now. The new baby would be lucky to have such helpful cousins, he said.

As Inga led the search for wood, the day continued to warm. That morning, at first light, sparse tiny snowflakes had gently sifted down from the sky, but the sun soon melted them. Spring was also time for hunters, since the seals would be migrating northward. But for the children this was especially a time for play after months indoors during the long winter. The women busied themselves preparing sealskins. Old Watching Eyes kept at her sewing with extraordinary industry, making clothes for the baby to come and for other children who had outgrown their clothing. Children were the Bear People's joy.

That afternoon Inga observed the children's glee at finding every useful stick on the shore. They proudly brought their treasures to Bearskin Girl to stack on the beach. This might be a game to them now, but they would learn their simple task was valuable to the community. Every precious bit of wood was needed. In their games they learned much. The children adored every new baby and made up games about babies. In some of them, they rescued the baby from danger with the raven as their ally.

Inga watched the raven stomp down the beach, pulling up fragments of wood here and there that the waves had buried in the sand. These the children added to their hoard.

"We might find something to make a toy for the new baby," one little boy said.

Inga advised, "Find shells for a rattle or a bone that can be carved."

"Will you carve it for us, *Mah-ee*?" a little girl asked.

"Laughing Friend will do it," Inga replied.

"You know how clever he is," Bearskin Girl agreed.

Inga did not call Laughing Friend by this nickname to the children. She had learned his true name years ago, but the one she had once made up for him fit him so well that she kept it secretly in her own mind.

Inga pondered the changes that were happening to her. She was growing up, too. She was sixteen now. She not only looked different – Old Watching Eyes had been busy sewing to keep up with her growing height – she also felt different. Exactly in what way she could not have explained. She felt quiet, serious, a bit dreamy. Like the earliest flowers that bloom even when the snow lies on the ground, she felt eager to blossom. Shining Eyes had wisdom worth learning and helped Silk Hair prepare for the baby. Inga often stood by to help and, thereby, shared in Shining Eyes' advice. When others were glad she was there to help, Inga felt the most grown up.

At last, Inga and Bearskin Girl bound the wood the

children had helped to gather, using strong hide cords. Silk Hair approached, summoning the children home. How radiant the young woman looked, Inga thought. Noisily the children hefted their bundles, glad to display their promising work, and Bearskin Girl led them home. Inga and Silk Hair watched the little ones totter over the snow-mottled grass, chuckling together at the sight.

When Inga remained alone again, Laughing Friend appeared and waved from the bank above.

"*Mah-ee!*" he called out. "We had good luck." Four older boys crowded round him. They held up the rabbits they had caught. Laughing Friend tossed his treasure into the arms of a companion and bolted down to the beach to meet Inga. His friends raced off, laughing and teasing.

Laughing Friend, too, was grown up. He was constantly busy with the tasks his elders found for him: hunting, fishing, mending boats, trading with distant villages, fashioning new implements with his skilful hands. He no longer merely rode along on an expedition, he led the younger boys. These days he regularly served in the hunting parties and spent most of his time with the older men, especially Whale Tooth, Cut Eye and Broken Smile, heeding their advice and absorbing their instruction.

Only now and then did he find time to walk with Inga and look out at the wide bays and misty peninsulas. Always he brought treats for the raven who welcomed him with affectionate sounds. He was the only person besides Inga to whom the raven would come. Laughing Friend still spent happy times playing "catch the stick" with this wily bird. When other boys tried to butt in, the raven would catch their sticks and drop them on their heads.

How tall and worthy Laughing Friend looked that afternoon, walking at her side! He had become much more than a friend. They rambled over the awakening land together, listening to the new birds screech and whistle. Earlier he had spied a meadow bursting with new flowers, he told her, where the air was sweet with their smell. She must see it, he said. They chattered along the route. Wind refreshed and sun warmed. Alongside them, the raven soared, cavorting in the springtime.

Inga said, "I know it is months off, but I must decide what gift to make for Silk Hair's baby. It must be something remarkable."

"You could weave a marvellous basket with your hair," he said, fingering the pale, flying strands.

"You," she replied, "could catch a bird and train it to tease, as well as you have taught our raven." He laughed.

"You are a skilled girl with a needle," he hinted. She had long ago given away her bone sewing needle and with it the piece of red woven cloth to hold it. The cloth had fascinated the Bear People, especially the women.

After a long, enjoyable stroll, they reached a headland and a flourishing spread of blue and yellow flowers. She knew the spot, but never had she seen it with such an abundance of blossoms. The flowers leaned this way and that in the brisk wind, like a flock of jolly birds.

Abruptly Laughing Friend stopped. He motioned to her to be silent. Inga followed his gaze to a scraggly tree at the edge of the bank. The raven clung to the topmost twig. She, too, recognized something troubling in the bird's appearance. His glance was fixed on something below. Inga whistled softly to him, in imitation of a songbird. The raven did not flinch in his observation.

"Seals?" Inga whispered to her companion. Laughing Friend gestured for her to remain there while he crept closer to the raven. She waited, curious. Soon, like the raven, the young man spied something on the shore that consumed his interest.

The raven suddenly croaked. "Gkkkk! Gkkkkk! Gkkkk!"

Inga heard voices muttering below. The raven fluttered from his perch just as some object whizzed past him, evidently tossed by an intruder below. A taunting shout followed.

Laughing Friend raced back, snatched her hand and tugged her away. They ran without a backward glance. Rounding a rocky crag, the pair huddled in its shadow.

"What did you see?" Inga whispered.

"Strangers," he said. After glimpsing through a crack in the rock and seeing nothing disquieting, he described what he had observed. There were three men, one carrying a club, the others knives. They were not of the Bear People. Of that he was certain. Inga was frightened. She listened to Laughing Friend's tense breathing. She knew he was afraid as well. Who were these strangers? What did they want? Were they stalking the village?

"What people do they come from?" she whispered finally.

He signalled that they must be silent. They waited for further sounds from the strangers or for noise of their departure. They heard nothing.

Laughing Friend whispered, "I do not think they saw me, but I am afraid they are looking for the village." When she tried to peer around the crag, he held her back.

"Could they be our people…but from a distant settlement?" she asked.

He frowned. "They are outsiders. And they do not have the manner of good men. I must warn everyone, but I can get there faster if I go alone. These intruders will not find you if you stay hidden and silent. Do not come out until I return." He motioned to a hollow behind the cliff where she could crouch unseen. "The raven will stay and guard you."

She grasped his arm. "How can you be sure they are not of our people?"

He bit his lip. "For one thing, they have a strange boat: slim as a fish and made of wood, not skin."

Inga drew in a startled breath.

He whispered, "I thought at first they were spirits, not people at all. But now," he added, his voice heavy with dread, "I think they may be of the Wolf People."

Inga sank to the ground, stunned. Wolf People! Norsemen! Her mind spun, circling like a bird high up in the sky caught in a stream of conflicting winds. Before she could stop him, Laughing Friend crawled out of the hiding place and disappeared. The wind helped conceal the sounds of his departure.

The raven hopped to the rock high above her and stared out with his bright, inquisitive eyes, seeing everything she could not see.

Wolf People! Those from whom she was lost years ago had returned. Her eyes rested on the strip of hide around her wrist and the feathers and shells around her neck, her hair flying loose and free. Would these people regard her as one of their own if she pleaded with them to spare the village?

She had no chance to answer her own puzzled questions for suddenly a cry and a flurry of yelps and grunts filled the air. The raven burst into the air and away. His brash alarms mixed with the sounds of a skirmish.

Inga peered through the crack in the rocks and saw Laughing Friend struggling with two stalwart men. These men were thickly bearded and wore long tunics of heavy woven cloth. Roughly they dragged Laughing Friend down the bank, despite his frantic resistance. Inga crawled after them, and hid in a large clump of briars

A third man waited on the shore by a boat. The captors talked among themselves in gruff words. These words she recognized, words she had not heard spoken –

except in her own thoughts – for years. Yes, these were Norsemen, but they were ruffians, those whom her old Greenland neighbours would have regarded as outlaws – hard, tough men. Their language was not the same turn of speech as the tongue of the people of the Greenland settlements, but she understood it. According to their conversation, they were renegades who had left a band of treasure seekers after a dispute broke out among them. In that dispute the expedition's leader had been slain.

The third man gave Laughing Friend a cruel blow with his fist. He demanded to know the way to his village. The men took his ivory knife and his stone hatchet. He had been hunting, the strangers decided, probably far from home. They would take him captive and make him lead them to a village where they hoped to find bundles of fur to steal or, if not, demand ransom for this captive. Then they would kill him. They wondered if his people had gold.

They bound Laughing Friend with strong cords and threw him into their boat. Inga struggled with wrangling thoughts. Alone she could not save Laughing Friend. Should she run back to the village for help? The boat might then travel far out of sight, and one whom she held so dear might be lost forever. No! No! That must not happen.

Brusquely the outlaws launched their boat, but she had no boat to follow. There was one stroke of luck for Laughing Friend: the wind blew stubbornly against them, and the men could scarcely make headway with their paddles. She decided to follow along at the shore, as long as possible, making certain she was not seen. Perhaps she could find out the direction they were headed.

"Krrek, krrek, krrek, krrek," the raven cried, watching the boat gain speed. The men launched a small sail to gain power. Wherever the raven led her, she stumbled after him, for in many places she could not see the boat at all. Where the brush was thick or her way wended among the rocks, she looked to the bird to guide her. Each time she reached a clearing, she found the raven's sharp eye had not lost sight of the strangers. If only they followed the coast, she vowed to follow, however far they might go.

Crouching, running, crawling, Inga kept thinking of Laughing Friend. What could she do to save him if she did catch up with his captors? She knew there was nothing to be hoped from revealing her origins. That the Bear People were her friends, her family, would mean nothing. The strangers would not know Uncle Knut or the captain of her lost ship. Good men would be of no interest to these outlaws. Their greedy thoughts were their only allies.

Gratefully, she felt the wind strengthen, and yet the men chose to sail against it, tacking back and forth. This told her two things: they had a particular destination ahead, for despite the contrary wind they were determined on a course, and their progress westward would remain slow. Secondly, their destination had to be on the mainland and not an outlying island. Somewhere down the coast, their henchmen probably awaited. Together they hoped to gather enough wealth to impress those they had parted from in their quarrel. These men sought plunder, above all else, as a way to win passage back home.

All these thoughts whirled in her mind as the sky began to dim. Nearly exhausted, she climbed one more promontory. The raven was nowhere to be seen. The boat was gone. Panicked, she searched the direction she had come from, a stunted patch of woods, a steep, rocky bank. Had she lost the way? Overhead two stars glimmered, and in the west a brilliant orange stripe of sunlight slashed the purple gloom. She imagined Laughing Friend among those ruffians. Laughing Friend had been right to fear these Wolf People. If only she could explain that the Norsemen were not all like these outlaws.

"Kork, kork, kork, kork, kork!" The raven fluttered overhead like a bat.

"Yes, yes, I see you," she gasped with relief. The bird led her down a stony bank where animals had worn a path to the shore. Inga gripped twisted branches to keep herself from sliding on the loose stones. The raven led her on. Soon she saw light bobbing on the water's surface below and a clear strip of shoreline. She crawled at the last, fearful of being seen.

But the path did not lead to the outlaws. Instead she came to a clearing where a small rivulet travelled through rushes to the shore. She stared at the scene before her. The clearing was evidently the site of an abandoned hunting camp of the Bear People. Shreds of ruined skins hung from poles of bone and wood. Strewn over the sand she saw blackened stones from a fire, a broken knife, the head of a stone axe and other bits of tools. Most haunting of all, an eerie shadow fell from a huge rack of caribou antlers tied to a weathered pole. The shadow flickered as if it were the spirit of the dead animal come to curse this place. She remembered how Broken Smile had told her of his rescue by a caribou and after that the animal had been his helping spirit. Because of this he wore around his neck a small carved caribou made from ivory. Inga needed such a helping spirit now.

A feeling of dread lingered here. The Bear People would never have left behind their tools and their tents. Some skirmish had happened, and she could guess with whom the Bear People had struggled, further proof of the fear the Bear People and the Wolf People felt toward each other.

The raven swooped down and perched on the awful antlers. He stared across the bay. She saw it now, too. The glow of a fire painted the rocks at a spot beyond the curve of the cove. That was surely the camp of the outlaws, and the scouting raven had found it.

"You are my helping spirit," she told the raven.

What might the raven tell her of the means for rescuing her dear friend? If only she had the magic powers of a sorceress in the old Norse tales. She could change men to beasts or terrify them with a spell. But she had no such magic. Her thoughts reeled as she sought the secret she needed. Then her gaze wandered to the raven on his perch of antlers. He gave her inspiration through this ominous sight. She had to work quickly now.

Through the darkness, she soon made her way along the shore and circled cautiously behind the outlaws' camp, until she heard low, muttering voices. Between boulders and branches she saw fingers of fire and shadow leap, and heard the salty driftwood crackle. The henchmen of the captors had roasted a fragrant meal that their newly arrived fellows eagerly downed. Their hiding place was well chosen, she observed from behind the site. Surrounded by rocks and masked from the sea by a rising bank, the hollow spot was shielded from view on all sides. At the centre of the ring of boulders, near her and facing the sea, rose the most enormous of all the rocks, standing like a massive door to a fortress. The shadow behind this rock wall let her hide, so she could study them carefully.

Where was Laughing Friend? Gripped by fear, she listened closely to their talk as the men clustered together. She recognized a man with a long, fresh scar across his cheek: one of Laughing Friend's captors. He gestured across the hiding place, so she knew that, although she couldn't see her dear friend, their captive was alive, and somewhere across the ring, blocked from view by the enormous centre stone.

Whatever kind of Norsemen they were, she knew the

old stories they must have heard from their infancy, tales of ghosts and fortune tellers, sorcerers and spirit voices that came to men in their dreams. The shadows and the flickering fire danced around the hidden ring of stones. Once more, all that Grandmother had taught her would save her. Grandmother had sent the raven, and now Inga realized again that, from the land of the spirits, Grandmother still watched over her granddaughter.

Working quickly, Inga brought out the strips of hide she had cut from the old abandoned tents. At her feet sprawled wild vines and these, too, she cut. She wove their rambling length to her purpose. When everything she needed was ready, she waited. She knew she would have to wait as long as it took for the outlaws to nod off to sleep to the voice of the tempestuous wind. Hours passed. Somewhere an owl wailed. Finally came the time when, in their dreams, all that men fear creeps in.

From where she waited behind the enormous centre boulder, Inga crept until she could spy Laughing Friend. He sat against a boulder, his hands and feet bound. He hung his head in the manner of a sleepy, defeated prisoner. But this was only a mask. When the men dozed off, at last, he lifted his head and studied his surroundings.

Five men lay sleeping around the fire. No longer joking or boasting, they lay with their bellies full and their eyes closed. Two snored. One had thrown wood on the fire before stretching himself out flat on a rock. He was the last to nod off. The others had all fallen asleep leaning against each other beneath sheltering rocks. The fire fitfully sputtered and jumped up in the gusts of wind, wind that howled faintly among the great rocks.

Inga motioned to the raven. As easily as a breath, the bird landed on the ground near Laughing Friend. The young man dared not speak or even turn his head, in case one of his captors opened his eyes. He did not want to draw attention to the clever little messenger. Yet his eyes searched the hiding place and the darkness beyond it. Though he saw nothing, he knew the raven had come to warn him: be ready, the moment comes. In another instant, the raven had flown away in a flutter of leaves tossed by a breeze. Laughing Friend's eyes sparkled. He waited.

Like a blow of thunder, a sound ripped the silence. "Gkkk! Gkkk! Gkkk! Gkkk!" the raven screamed. Groggy, two of the outlaws tried to shrug off sleep. Another grunted.

"Gkkk! Gkkk! Gkkk! Gkkk!" came the alarm once more. The men shook their heads as if to shake out the sleepiness. They sat up, stared at each shadow. One grumbled and scrambled up on his knees. Another kicked a few sticks in the fire so the flames leapt up and hissed.

Then above them, upon the enormous centre boulder, its blank face rippling with a sorcery of shadows, they saw an astonishing and terrifying sight: a figure they had only imagined from ancient tales and drunken gossip. A young woman stood there high on the boulder above them, slender and pale-eyed like their own people, her long hair, the colour of the sun, frenzied and savage as it blew in the wind. Her shapely young body was draped in vines, twigs and flowers, as if she had risen up out of the earth itself. Now her arms stretched out and above her like opening wings.

There was no mistaking her identity, not to a Norseman! Crowning her floating hair, she wore a thick wreath of convoluted vines and branches. With horror they saw protruding from this wreath something hideous: claw-like antlers rising from her head. One man shrieked. Another stumbled to his feet. "The Elf-Maiden," one groaned. Others, too, whispered this awful name.

Suddenly the raven pounced upon the supposed Elf-Maiden's shoulder. "Gkkk! Gkkk! Gkkk! Gkkk!" His warning pierced the night. His black eyes flamed with magic light from the reflected fire.

In terror, the men heard the Elf-Maiden speak to them, and her words, even in this savage land so far from home, were in their own tongue!

"*Fort! Fort!*" she wailed. "Quickly! Quickly! You have mistaken your way!" Her tapered fingers pointed to each of them in turn. "*Reise bort!* Depart now!" she commanded. "Go away! Go! Never return to this land if you hope to save your lives! *Forsiktig! Forsiktik!* Beware!"

The ruffians scrambled to their feet and, falling over each other, raced to their boats. Their shouts — more distant as they fled over the water — unravelled in the wind. In an instant, Inga was at Laughing Friend's side, and, once freed, the young man fled with her into the darkness.

When Inga once again awakened in the warm turf house in the village, filled with the familiar sights and sounds of the Bear People, she smelled something cooking on the fire. To soothe the raw coolness of the day, she filled a stone bowl for herself. As she ate, the happy sounds of the children at play outside drifted to her. Then something rustled at the entrance. Laughing Friend entered.

"For you, *Mah-ee*," he said gently. He held up his gift: a new necklace of perfect white feathers from a winter owl. He had attached each feather with fine sinew to the hide ring. Inga touched the white downy plumes.

"It's beautiful," she said, standing to try it on. In the firelight, she winced at the red, raw bruises around his wrists where he had been bound. She slipped on the necklace. Her gaze rested on this beautiful gift as if she had been given a ringlet of stars. When she looked up, Laughing Friend had gone. She saw through the doorway that the men still gathered outside, solemnly listening to Laughing Friend as he related the story of the Wolf People and his capture and escape.

Old Watching Eyes hobbled in and sat in the light of the doorway to sew. She carried a skin bag with some other garments folded inside, but her immediate interest was a tiny garment trimmed with fur that she sewed for

Silk Hair's expected baby. Inga cast her eyes away from the old woman. She had recognized for some time that the secret garments the old woman kept in the bag were warm clothes of fur and hide that the old woman made, not for another, but for herself. These were for the long journey to the land of the dead. Watching Eyes seemed to know that her journey neared.

"Gaagh!" Watching Eyes scoffed. "This old needle! I might as well sew with one of my own teeth!"

At once Inga fetched something from her storage corner. She brought her leather purse to the doorway. "Here," she said. "This is for you." She gave the old woman the small whetstone she had found long ago when the purse had washed ashore. "Sharpen your needle on that stone; it will be as good as new." Watching Eyes fingered the fine honing stone. "Keep it," Inga told her. "It should belong to a skilful seamstress like you."

"Thank you, my dear," Watching Eyes replied quietly. She blinked away a tear and began to sharpen her needle.

Before Inga put the purse back in its place, she peered inside. Yes, it was empty now. Everything had been given away. Good, she thought. In some puzzling way, the empty purse gave her a sense of relief.

Part 4

*At the dawn of the new world, the earth came
forth from the sea, green and refreshed.
Baldur left the kingdom of the dead
and came to join the younger gods,
survivors of the terrible destruction.
The former world had disappeared,
but they hoped to reign over a better one.*

The Deception of Gylfi

Chapter Ten

A Carved Figurine

A hunting camp, Newfoundland

Revellers roused the summer night with song. Two days before the hunters departed, Silk Hair's baby boy had been born. Now, even here in the hunting camp, merry spirits continued. Inga stood alone in the darkness on a bank above the shore, spellbound by another song: the night chant of the sea. Compared to the revelry of those gathered by the tents at the campfire, this chant was lulled and hushed, yet just as enchanting. Here she welcomed the cool night breeze.

The night was full of peace. For days stormy weather with driving winds had beaten the coast. Some feared the winter was coming early. Ridges of seaweed lay stranded on shore, and in the darkness looked like sleeping seals. All afternoon shorebirds had strutted the beach, searching for delicious treasures surrendered by the storms. In the darkness now, she could hear the laughter of those circling the macabre light and shadow of the fire. They spoke of the other hunters who had gone north in search of the caribou. They spoke of their own hopes of finding seals migrating southward. Laughing Friend sat contentedly among them. Some were younger boys who felt privileged to accompany Whale Tooth's expedition, boys who preferred the nimble, skin-covered boats and the tang of the salt winds to the northern treks, for theirs was a sea people.

The raven, on Inga's shoulder, never liked these night-time strolls. Night was owl time. But he would not let Inga wander alone and clung fast with his wiry feet, his beak so close it brushed her cheek.

"We won't stay long," she promised the raven, "only long enough to let this breeze sweep away our sleepiness." Inga had no intention of missing the campfire gathering of story and song. But there was something odd moving around her heart tonight, a nameless happiness like a young fledgling straying from the nest, full of wonder in its new world. Her life was easy now, every day filled with little joys like the millions of stars that give joy to the dark heavens. The future pledged more gladness to come. She was not afraid to leave girlhood behind. She awaited her new life as a woman with buoyant impatience.

Everyone had admired Laughing Friend's fanciful gift for Silk Hair's baby. From a carved wooden ring, toys hung like icicles, colourful and curious objects on strings of sinew: polished purple and yellow shells, carved wooden animals stained with berry juice, coins that Inga had given him long ago and small bones tied up in fine nets so they rattled as they swayed. The baby could watch these toys spin as they hung over his head. Inga felt deeply pleased to see Laughing Friend win the praise of the village. The young man was not the keenest of hunters, a bit too dreamy to be a good tracker, but he could bring beauty into a life that could be harsh, and he possessed both kindness and wisdom. She glanced over at his silhouette by the fire.

Inga's gift was a basket woven in a pattern Blue Shell had taught her. She added one touch of her own: among the grasses and rushes she had woven threads pulled from her own cloak, the merry yellow thread that she had once dyed with flowers and the warm brown dyed with nuts. Laughing Friend admired the gift, and Shining Eyes had pronounced her work a splendid display of skill.

On her shoulder the raven mumbled restlessly. "Why are you glum, little one?" she teased. "Not the centre of attention now? Is that it?" The bird muttered. Was he speaking of the great dancing lights overhead in the northern sky? They had appeared for two nights now. She watched the leaping green, pink and white light frolicking above her in the black sky. Laughing Friend had said the lights greeted the new baby. Whale Tooth thought the lights a sign the child had a remarkable destiny as a leader among the Bear People. The dancing lights were so bright that most of the stars remained hidden behind their radiance. The night tingled with beauty.

To the east, Inga saw one lone star, small but clear. That star might also be a sign of good fortune for the baby. She had noticed that Laughing Friend found pleasure in the prospect of teaching his young cousin about the world they lived in. As tiny and fragile as the baby was, all the taller and wiser Laughing Friend felt himself to be. He strutted, almost like the raven. One day Laughing Friend would be a father and teach his own children. Her cheeks grew warm at this thought. Was she to be a part of that dream? That low bright star could also be a sign for Laughing Friend, she thought. He was a man now. The night sang of portents for them all.

The raven sputtered suddenly. Inga listened closely to the night but heard no owl's call, no rustle in the brush. She wondered if the raven could hear an owl's flight, even though for people, the owl was the silent flyer of the birds.

"Yours are owl dreams," she scoffed gently. "That's all these owls are." Yet she peered around her cautiously. Had she stepped too close to a precipice? Was there a sound of approaching steps she had missed? She heard and saw nothing. "Owl dreams," she whispered to her own skittish heart. There was no place for unhappiness there.

Faraway, scarcely above the horizon, the small star burned with a pure light. The vigil of this light soothed her. "We must remember this spot exactly, so we may come and visit this star," she said to the raven. She knew that coast across the channel, sprinkled with rocks along its shore. She and Laughing Friend had paddled along it, watching birds fly up from the grass. "Too bad you are so crabby tonight," she said. "The night is beautiful, but we will go back."

The raven refused to be comforted. He grumbled, although Inga headed over the dark land toward the warmth of the fire.

The light of approaching day had not yet stirred the sky the next morning when a dream awakened Inga, a startling dream. Years had passed since she had last dreamt of her forgotten childhood home, and this was an odd dream, at that. In the dream, eagles circled all day, and later, while she walked out on the land at twilight, she found feathers scattered on the grass, black feathers. As the dream went on, she frantically searched for the raven. But when she leaned to pick up the unmoving, bloodied body of the bird she found, the raven opened his eyes and flashed a look at her. Nothing else moved, only the startling black eyes. She shuddered at the remembrance of the vision. Those flashing eyes left Inga deeply frightened, both in her dream and in the instant of awakening.

"Why have I had this peculiar dream?" she whispered. She blinked, scanning the shadowy tent draped with bearskins. The raven was not there. Softly as a secret, she slipped outside.

In the bleakness before sunrise, the sea was visible only as a shadow. The whole world lay still, as if both land and sea held their breath. "*Ravn?*" she whispered. She spun completely around. There, at the top of a tent pole, she saw him. Utterly still, the raven fixed his eye on something distant. Inga saw it now, too. The star, the same low star, hung in the east. It had not moved during the night. *Stars move*, Inga thought to herself. For a time, she simply stood there.

Then, spellbound, she could not stop her feet from striding over the damp grass toward the upturned boats on the shore. Deftly she righted a boat and slid it into the calm water. As she dipped her paddle into the sleeping sea, Inga scarcely noticed the raven drift down from the sky and land on the prow. The star soon fell out of sight behind the land, but she headed in the direction where earlier its light shone.

"I must know," she murmured.

Oblivious of the unseen animals scurrying up from the water's edge, Inga paddled onward. She did not notice that, before long, the dark folds of water rippling behind her pointed toward a second boat following her in the distance. The tall youth in that craft kept his eyes fastened on her as he paddled quietly. The raven, too, paid little heed to what lay behind them. The spell enchanted him, too, and his eyes remained fixed on the dark, watery path ahead.

As slyly as a ghost, the light of day crept into the sky. After some while, Inga passed the spot where years ago a boat she had been meant to guard slid down the slick mud, and she had nearly been swept out to sea trying to retrieve it. There! Was that the jutting rock she had tried to catch as a terrified, young girl, helpless to steer the lost boat ashore?

Each point of land fell back to reveal a change in the scene. The land became more open, but the star did not reappear. She knew that before long the sun would peer over the sea's edge and ignite the sky. The star would fade.

Yes, she remembered this coastline, remembered, too, what lay beyond. This story she had long ago stopped telling herself. The light was probably no more than the campfire of a wandering hunting party. But perhaps that was what she needed now, the mere sight of that abandoned Norse camp once more, a memory of a world now dead to her. Her people were the Bear People, and like bears they were strong, enduring, and loving to their children. She had made her home among them, and that vision of a lost world must slip away while the life she had embraced moved happily forward.

Then, crossing round a headland, she saw the star's light again, flickering clearly. The light drew her closer, like a sorcerer's spell. Her boat angled closer to shore, and for an instant the starry light fell out of sight again. From the corner of her eye she caught sight of the boat behind her, gliding closer over the smooth water but always lingering at a distance. She knew well who followed her through the mysterious dawn. Yet she could not stop. Would he understand what was happening to her?

"I must see," she whispered to the raven who eyed the water ahead.

Her boat nimbly rounded the point. There were the same shallows, exposing the curve of the sandbar where her wandering craft had slipped aground. The smell of fire reached her. "Ah, a fire," she whispered, "no more than that." Then from somewhere near she heard the chime of a hammer clanging, clanging against iron. Her head fell back as if struck by a blow. She felt her breath choking. How long had it been since she had heard that music, the rhythm of hammer on iron? This was her star. She saw it now: a fire burning in a forge!

Yet another wonder awaited, so stunning that she gripped the boat to steady herself: straight ahead at the mouth of the inlet, an impossible vision, no ghost this time. A fine ship anchored in the deeper water and bobbed in the swell of an incoming tide. This was a Norse ship whose voyagers must have taken refuge here during the recent storms.

Mindlessly, she heard her little boat slip into the pebbly shallows. A new light drew her on, the simple glow in the doorway of the longhouse. The door stood open. A ladder leaned against one end of the house where someone had been mending the roof. The raven fluttered ahead, for he knew her direction already, and landed on the crest of the longhouse roof. No figurehead above the fierce waves by a warrior's ship could have looked bolder than the raven.

Somehow she found herself there instantly, standing at the threshold. It was all there this time: an array of supplies removed from the ship for safekeeping, richly coloured woven cloths hanging on the walls, barrels in the corner, iron pots and brass spoons at the fire, a game board atop a stout chest ornamented with brass fittings, the game pieces ready for the players to take up.

A strongly built man sat on a stool with his back to her. In the opposite corner an old, white-haired man packed a chest with supplies, folding a thick red cloth and placing it inside with care. A young woman raked the embers of a dying fire. Yes, these were Norse people.

Suddenly she reminded herself of the way they would see her: a girl in a fur and hide garment, a necklace of white feathers around her neck, barefoot, her tangled hair flowing around her sunburnt face. The raven swooped down to her shoulder, glaring at the occupants of the room. From behind her, outside in the brush, a movement caught her eye, a young man sneaking behind a boulder. She knew who hid there, watching. Yes, she knew. But she had to go on.

Inga stared at the people in the great room of the longhouse. But the words of her childhood stuck in her throat. The remembered sounds felt strange and outlandish to her tongue. Was it that she hesitated to speak at all? Should she run away? Then the woman at the fire dropped her spoon, which clanked and sizzled on the hot stones. The old man packing the chest cried out, and the sitting man near her leapt to his tall height and whirled around. The three of them gaped at Inga.

Hoarse words stumbled from her throat. "It is I... Inga...Sigurdsdottir." Something else thumped to the floor. She spoke her name once more, and its sound was a ghost to her ears.

"A spirit!" the old man warned in a whisper.

"*Nei*," the tall man spoke up. "Inga...Inga. Is it you?"

She mumbled, her tears brimming, "I saw the light... from the forge." The raven swooped up to the rafters and let out at an enormous croak. Instinctively the Norse people cringed at the sight of this strange bird – but only for an instant – for the figure at the threshold was compelling.

The tall man continued, "Inga...you are alive!"

From the corner, the old man called out a warning again. The tall man stepped into the light of the morning sun aslant in the doorway, replying, "*Nei*, this is no ghost, Ivar. This is my sister's child, Inga."

"Uncle Knut!" Inga cried. Although his face was lined and his hair speckled with grey, she could see now the familiar eyes, the sage smile. She ran into his arms. Her uncle's tears fell upon her like a blessing.

"We thought you had drowned," he murmured.

The language of her childhood came forth, but only clumsily, as if her mouth were full of pebbles. "I...the ship...the ship was wrecked...the storm," Inga stammered, "and Grandmother...Grandmother..." She could not utter these painful words, even now.

"Yes, we know," he answered solemnly. "Three survived to tell the story, but Elina Eiriksdottir was not among them. No, four survived, for here you are." He leaned her head back with a tender hand. "I would not mistake those eyes! God be praised!"

"I thought I was all alone," Inga exclaimed, weeping.

Her uncle explained, "The others came upon a *skraeling* boat and made their way northward, sheltering along the coast of Markland until another ship happened by. They, too, thought they were the only survivors."

He stared at her as if, indeed, she were a ghost, a wonderful ghost. "Margret, bring her something to eat," he told the young woman. To Inga, he added, "This woman came from Iceland with your mother. How your mother grieved for you. Now what joy she will have." A fragrant piece of cheese was thrust into her hands. "Ah, but she will not know her little daughter, so tall and strong!"

Her mother! Inga struggled to remember her mother's face, but only a blur of pale hair came to her mind. Go back? It was unthinkable.

"Uncle Knut," she stammered, "I...I cannot."

"You are all grown up," her uncle said, stroking her hair. "I can hardly believe that you are here...alive." He shook his head in disbelief. "The good spirits have been with you."

Inga's words tumbled out. "Grandmother's ghost has been with me. She saved me. She sent me this raven to guide me." She held out her arm and in an instant the raven glided down to her wrist. He nibbled the cheese. Her onlookers laughed.

"A spirit bird!" her uncle exclaimed. He cast his eyes to the floor. "I don't doubt that Elina Eiriksdottir would work such miracles from the land beyond."

Inga hurried to explain. "She led me to safety when I was lost. She brought me to the help I needed."

Was *he* hiding nearby? she wondered, glancing out the door. Or had he fled from these alien people? She turned to her uncle, begging with her eyes and with her heart. "Uncle, my friends saved me…the friends Grandmother brought me to when I was alone and hungry and surely doomed to die."

She stepped to the doorway and into the light. Yes, a shadow bolted into the brush and slipped away toward the shore. Suddenly, the raven burst out the open doorway and followed him. Inga knew she must go, too. The faraway world of the past was lost long ago. She must flee!

Her uncle's hand rested gently on her shoulder. "We are preparing to depart," he explained. "Come." He led her inside once more.

"You must meet them before you go," Inga insisted, "my village…my friends…"

Her uncle straightened his tall figure, startled. "Do you mean there are others yet who survived?"

"God be praised," cried the old man.

"Let us go to them at once," her uncle declared.

"I will call the men from the forge," Margret, the young woman, said.

"No," Inga protested, begging through her tears. If only they would understand. "I have not been alone here, because the Bear People, the people of this land, found me and took me in. I have lived as one of their own children would live—"

"The *skraelings!*" the young woman gasped.

"They were kind to me," Inga plunged on. They must understand!

"*Skraelings!*" her uncle exclaimed. "Yet here you are. Alive!" He rushed past her into the yard. "I think I saw someone crawling in the brush, hiding!" He cupped his hands and yelled toward the forge. "Tomas! Halfdan! Einarr! Come! There are savages about!" He whirled back toward the old man now at the doorway. "Ivar, go quickly out to the ship and bring every man with you. Tell them to bring their weapons."

"No! No!" Inga insisted, rushing outside to her uncle's side. "They are good—"

"Never trust a *skraeling!*" the old man warned. His brow was fiercely contorted.

"We may trade with them," her uncle growled, "but we cannot trust them."

Margret cried, "Brutal people, savage heathens. To capture a mere child and keep her prisoner all these years!"

Inga felt her world falling apart like a star tumbling from the night sky. They must not harm the people of her village. She must stop them! Then her deliverance — the deliverance of the Bear People — struck her. She knew what she must do.

"No, there is no one out there," she insisted, gripping her uncle's arm. "That was only a fox in the brush. I saw it earlier. The *skraelings* are far from here, Uncle. I set out all alone, while it was still night. It is better that we depart this very moment." She urged passionately, "They have no swift ships such as yours. Is it not a wiser course that we not risk a single life? We will be in no danger if we go now, this minute. What would be gained by attacking them? You were ready to embark. Let us go! All of us! Now!"

The raven appeared from the sky, alighting atop the ladder and filling the air with his clattering call. Three young men, dashing over the rocks from the forge, stopped to stare at this peculiar omen.

Her uncle held up a hand to stop the men. He frowned. "Inga is right. If we can avoid bloodshed, let us do so. We have lost too many in this strange land already."

Margret shuddered. "Yes, let us go home, away from this heathen place!"

Her uncle ordered the men from the forge, "Make haste! Bring our provisions to the shore. We depart at once! Ivar, bring the boats." He turned to his niece. "Inga, you have spoken wisely. Come!"

"Grawwwkk!" the raven croaked.

"If the bird is a spirit," the old man spoke up, "I think he is a good one. He wants us to go peacefully." He nodded to Uncle Knut. "We will bring the boats at once."

At least, Inga thought, I have the raven. They would be friends forever. She turned to her uncle. "I must first bring my boat up and hide it, so they will not find it." She fled from his embrace.

Was she too late? Was she not to have one more glimpse of the one of all the Bear People who was dearest to her? As she darted into the brush a hand dragged her to the ground. Laughing Friend's hand covered her mouth to muffle her scream.

"*Mah-ee*," he gasped. "You have escaped. Quick, we can go this way. I have hidden your boat behind those rocks. Come." His face, with its shining dark eyes and handsome brow, was marvellous in her gaze. Yes, she would have this to remember, a glimpse of one whom it was agony to lose. She could hold on to that vision forever.

He muttered, "We will get the others and chase these Wolf People away. They will not harm you, *Mah-ee!*"

"No, they won't harm me," she whispered, gently drawing his hand away. "But they will harm our friends and family. They have bold weapons, and they are full of fear, as you are, my dearest friend."

Laughing Friend frowned. "What do you mean?"

Inga spoke with words heavy with sadness. "There is only one way: I must leave this land with them."

His eyes widened at this impossible idea. "No!"

Inga pleaded quietly, "If I go with you, these people will search for the hunting camp. And they will find it. They might find the village, as well. Our people must not know they have come, for they, too, will be frenzied with fear. We — you and I together — we can save them both."

Reluctantly, she told him what she now understood. "Now that the Wolf People know I am here, they will not leave without me. They are too frightened to see the people of our village for what they are, not ferocious beasts at all, and our people are too terrified to see these folk as anything but hungry wolves." She concluded, "But we can save them from each other."

She took his hands in her own and held them close to her. "There is no other way." She looked into his rigid, mute face. "Think of those you love. Is there one among them whose life you would willingly lose?" She nodded toward the encampment. "One of those men is my uncle, and he tells me that my mother is still living and a woman who is her friend is here among them. Would you kill them while I look on?"

Laughing Friend said nothing. He stared into her face as if, otherwise, he might forget it. "But you will come back, later?"

This she could not answer. "I do not know. I hope so."

He vowed, "When our people are friends, I will come and find you. You are not of the Wolf People. You never were, not to me."

A summons rang out from up on the hill. "I must go," she said. She got to her feet as the raven lighted on her shoulder with a warning croak.

Inga parted the branches before her face, ready to plunge through them. Then she stopped. She turned around and held out her arm. The raven hopped down to her wrist. Once more she faced Laughing Friend. "Wait. The raven must go home with you." She held out her precious little companion. "If I cannot stay, he can. He, too, belongs here. With you."

Reluctantly, Laughing Friend raised his arm. The raven jumped over to him and looked back at Inga, puzzled.

She smiled. "Yes, this is right. Perhaps some day we will all be one people, the People of the Earth."

She turned back to the brush, ducked her head and slipped away. She did not look back again but heard Laughing Friend speak to the bird as, no doubt, he held it from flight.

"Raven, stay by me," the young man commanded.

Inga saw no more of her raven or the young man, and soon the broad sail of the Norse ship billowed with the morning light as the craft sped through the waves. The mist had disappeared. The day was full of beauty. She stood in the stern as the land of the Bear People retreated, glistening in green and gold, light and shadow. Her uncle stood at her side, his hand warmly clasping her shoulder.

"You *are* Inga," he said. "Inga Sigurdsdottir." Then he left her to turn his mind to the ship's course. The banks and coves, the islands and scattered rocks grew smaller. The sea widened in every direction.

Inga murmured to herself, "I am Inga. I am *Mah-ee*." She stared at the sea and the unravelling wake. "I am Inga Sigurdsdottir. I am *Mah-ee*."

As the ship left the danger of rocks and shoals and entered the open sea, its passengers settled down comfortably. The old man sat near Inga as she stood watching the sea-path behind them. He plucked forth a scrap of wood and began to whittle a figurine, as he often did to pass the time. He carved her as she stood, watching the last speck of land on the horizon and, afterwards, the brilliant surface of the sun-gilded sea when land could be seen no more. He carved her, as she stood there, except that, remembering the magical bird that had earlier accompanied her – a bright-eyed spirit from another world – he placed a raven upon her shoulder.

Acknowledgements

The ingredients combining to create any novel are far too numerous to list and often are assembled over a long period. The inspirations for *Raven, Stay by Me* include a ship voyage to Europe, sailing from Montreal up the St. Lawrence through the Gulf to the Atlantic, when we were obliged to crawl for days through late-breaking icebergs and pack ice, an impressive sight that inevitably conjured up visions of ancient navigators. A course taken at Trinity College, Dublin, exploring medieval archaeology, let me see Norse artefacts and ruins of Norse coastal sites in Ireland with my own eyes. Beyond these beginnings, I am indebted to numerous books, visual records, scholarly articles, and ancient texts. But a few merit special mention for their invaluable help.

I have benefited richly from the writings of Bernd Heinrich on ravens, particularly *Mind of the Raven* (Harper Collins, 1999) and *Ravens in Winter* (Vintage, 1991) in my portrait of the raven's habits and irrepressible character.

As no other texts can be, the great Sagas of travel to the New World were my lifeline to a distant and enigmatic time. The Sagas vividly describe the early Norse mindset, its world of presences and spirits and its complex kinship with Nature. I have been guided by this depiction of the New World, of encounters with the people the Sagas call *skraelings* and the accounts of the mutual distrust between the indigenous people and the Norse. The Poetic Edda and the Prose Edda, quoted in the section headings, also helped shape my sense of this ancient world.

The archaeological exploration of the L'Anse aux Meadows site, in northern Newfoundland, begun under the direction of archaeologist Anne Stine Ingstad (Helge and Anne Stine Ingstad, *The Viking Discovery of America*, Checkmark, 2001) provided invaluable insight into the Norse presence, the physical reality of the Norse sites and the remaining artefacts. I am grateful also for the resources of the Newfoundland Museum and Parks Canada, whose archives of scholarly work, especially on the native peoples of Atlantic Canada and on the Norse and the geographic setting, were indispensible.

L.W. van Keuren is a writer of fiction and drama for children, often with a strong connection to history. Professor Emerita from California University of Pennsylvania, she taught literature and creative writing for many years before becoming a full-time writer. She received her Ph.D. in English from the University of Delaware and also studied abroad in Austria, Spain, and Ireland. The author makes her home in mid-coast Maine with six cats and a flock of geese.